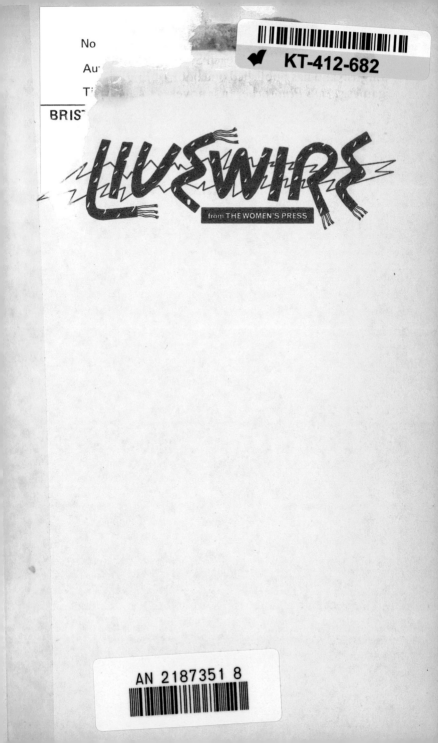

LIVEWIRE

from THE WOMEN'S PRESS

Christine Purkis used to teach Secondary School English and has published one book of English Learning games. *Peta's Pence* is her first novel.

Christine Purkis
Peta's Pence

For Mopsa

With special thanks to Sue Reid for editing this book

Livewire Books for Teenagers
First published by The Women's Press Limited 1990
A member of the Namara Group
34 Great Sutton Street, London EC1V 0DX

British Library Cataloguing in Publication Data
Purkis, Christine
  Peta's pence,
  I. Title
  823.914 [J]

  ISBN 0-7043-4923-X

Typeset in 11pt Bembo
by MC Typeset Ltd, Gillingham, Kent.
Printed and bound by BPCC Hazell Books Ltd,
Member of BPCC Ltd, Aylesbury, Bucks, England

July 1987

'Oh! Look!'

The elderly woman caught her breath, stood still on the gravel path and tugged at her sister's arm.

'What dear?'

'Over there!' she whispered, pointing a gloved finger towards the corner of the graveyard. 'Under that yew tree!'

'Oh yes,' replied the other calmly. 'It's only a boy.'

'But . . . it's one of those ruffians, those long-haired boys that drive motorbikes! Look at his jacket.'

'He's not doing anything that I can see dear,' her sister said soothingly.

'Desecrating! I've seen it on the television,' she wailed.

'Nonsense dear. He's sitting there doing no harm. Perhaps he's lost someone too,' she added reproachfully.

Sniffing at the lavender water she had dabbed on the corner of her handkerchief before leaving the house, the younger sister took a firmer grip of her bunch of honeysuckle and weigela. She'd clipped them that very morning from the bush in the front garden. How pleased Albert would be to receive the fruits of his labours! Could it really have been such a short time ago, the autumn, that he'd pruned all the bushes in the garden so savagely? Too savagely they had thought at the time, and told him so.

'What do you know about it, eh? You girls!' he had said with that disparaging sneer on his face which

1

always annoyed her so much. Still, not really the time to be thinking such thoughts. She tried to relax her jaw that had set rigidly, and always did when she thought of him.

'Just you wait and see,' Albert had told them. The spring buds had proved him right too!

Somehow she had lagged behind again. Her sister was waiting for her.

'Come along dear.' She took her arm and guided her over the gravel, through the grey stone slabs, to that part of the cemetery where the earth lay exposed and pink and mounded, where fresh flowers lay drooping and dying into the soil.

Peta hadn't heard their footsteps; hadn't felt herself observed. If she had, she'd just have sighed with the boredom of it all.

She sat cross-legged at the foot of a small grave. Overhead, the dark bough of the yew lifted and swayed in the breeze. She sat facing the gravestone. Behind it there was a dark holly hedge alive with gossiping sparrows.

Peta turned her eyes back to the little grave. Grass grew there, thick and green and the headstone had already mellowed so the name was not so distinct or easy to read now:

PETER PIPER
JESUS CALLED HIM 15:1:71
AGED THREE YEARS
'SUFFER THE LITTLE CHILDREN'

Peta suddenly hurled a small piece of gravel which hit the stone with a small plink.

'I hate that stupid thing – 'Suffer the little children' – what's that supposed to mean?' She said it vehemently, but in her head, perhaps to him.

She wouldn't have known what it meant either. But there again, it couldn't have been his idea. Probably the *only* line she knew. It *must* have been her doing – sick like the name. She smiled.

'Well,' this time she spoke out loud but softly, 'I'm off – at long last. I've finally done it. Thought you ought to know.' She stretched out a hand and lightly trailed her fingers over the tips of the grass.

What was left, down there, under her hand? Two foot of cloying clay, threaded with roots, tunnelled with long garden worms and little black beetles and blind, colourless creatures with hundreds of legs; a wooden lid, probably rotten by now; perhaps there were still shreds of colourless material clinging to . . . bones. Surely the worst must be over; just bones, little yellow, earthy bones.

Peta sprang up suddenly, took a deep breath, stretched her arms above her head. She stood still for a second longer, and then turned and stomped off over the turf and down the path, her big black boots scuffing the gravel.

The two sisters, standing by their brother's grave, watched her for a while. The elder turned back and bowed her head. The younger stared after the retreating figure, puzzling over the hunched shoulders and the long angry stride. There was something strong there, and yet a suggestion of pain too, but not the pain of sadness you might expect to find in this place.

Peta had seen her brother, just the once. Impossible, she knew, but she *had* seen him and she thought about it again now as she marched past all the other sleepers. She'd been very young at the time, three perhaps, and she remembered waking one night to a strange sound.

What is it? . . . What is it? The flame of the candle

3

night-light still burning making funny dancing shadows on the ceiling . . . don't like them . . . sit up! . . . Who is it? . . . in the corner . . . not a shadow, no definitely not a shadow . . . Don't know him. Don't think I know him . . . Hey! Opening my toy cupboard! They're my bricks! Mine. A red one and a blue one! Mine! . . . Jumping out of bed . . . running . . . snatching . . . shouting . . . Mine! Mine! Mummy there in the doorway, in her nightie . . . My bricks! He's got my bricks! Mummy screaming then running too and calling my name . . . my name! Peta! Peta! but softly not crossly as if she wanted to cuddle and love . . . Mummy on her knees by the toy cupboard, running to me . . . still calling my name . . . trying to clamber on her lap to get close, skin close . . . no, no, away! Pushed away! Away into the cold!

Mummy standing, voice distant, icy, 'Go to bed! Go to sleep! You've had a dream.' Then her screaming: 'It was a dream!' and running away sobbing and sobbing . . . and the bed so cold. Don't know what he looked like but I know I saw him. Maybe he was golden and curly like the photo on the mantlepiece in the living room or maybe darker and more solemn like the one in the silver frame next to her bed.

Now, when Peta reached the lichgate she didn't look back, but stood for another moment facing the busy suburban street, the rush of traffic and the valley below, the hills and the blue horizon. It took no more than a moment to decide that it was there that she wanted to be, and not in the cold dead world behind her back.

January 1971

A big black limousine came mournfully up the hill, emerging from the blurring smoke pall into the clearer, colder air. It drew up at the gate and the chauffeur jumped out, slamming his door behind him.

Another sleek black car drew up behind the first. The back door opened and two black-stockinged legs were swung elegantly round. The chauffeur hastened dutifully to assist. The young woman stood for a moment and there was something disorientated about her stance. A little black velvet pill-box hat was perched on her head with a low veil covering her face. She stood staring into the far distance, at nothing.

She shivered and pulled her coat around her legs. The fabric was straining over her chest and belly; she felt as though she would burst out any minute, like a butterfly from a chrysalis. Buttons would fly in all directions – they would lie spattered on the pavement like dark drops of rain. How absurd. She almost smiled. Perhaps if she kept thinking of the butterfly, that might be a way of getting through it all. The veil was tickling the end of her nose. She blew gently and saw a faint fluttering in front of her eyes. Her mother had lent her the hat, ridiculously out of date she knew, but she felt a kind of safety behind this frail curtain. No one could see her eyes. She'd half expected to see the world cut into diamonds, but strangely it looked almost normal, a trifle greyer perhaps, and fuzzy at the edges.

The church bell of St Andrew's started to toll. It

5

reverberated in her heart and suddenly, unexpectedly, a huge sob rose in her throat and nearly overwhelmed her.

No! No! Be somewhere else! Another time! A safe time! Long ago . . . not waiting . . . not standing . . . . running . . . yes, running across a field . . . running fast with the wind in her hair . . . Dad standing there, his boots lost in the celandines and dandelions and buttercups . . . flying her kite, the one he had made her . . . wearing her red wellingtons . . . watching it dip and swoop over the whole sky.

She was staring intently up at the clouds when the vicar approached, so she did not see him; neither did she see the little coffin being pulled out of the limousine.

'Mrs Piper, Mrs Piper!' the vicar had to repeat her name.

'Ah! Vicar.' She smiled breathlessly. He looked rather taken aback.

'Is Mr Piper not with you?'

'I wanted to drive here alone,' she explained.

At that moment a battered blue Vauxhall drew up on the opposite side of the road. Tom jumped out first, waved rather frantically at his wife and then turned to help his mother-in-law, his brother Jerry at the wheel.

'I'll go and park,' Jerry called.

'Righty ho!'

Frances turned away.

'I'd have been all right by myself,' she thought bitterly, nibbling at her lower lip.

Out of the corner of her eye she was aware of her mother hovering uncertainly at the gate and dabbing at her cheeks. She was wearing her second-best hat, dark felt with the brim swept back away from her face.

'She looks ridiculous too!' thought Frances cruelly. 'She wants me to speak but I won't.'

'OK love?' Tom's breath smelt of whisky.

She nodded, turning away from him.

He shuffled his feet and cleared his throat nervously.

6

'What happens now Vicar?' He needed to talk, keep busy.

If she opened her mouth now, the wave might spill out and carry them all away.

The little group of mourners threaded its way through the old burial stones leaning at odd angles, cracked with time, past stone angels and marble crosses, plastic flowers, inappropriate somehow, and so vulgar, so *vulgar*.

They stood on raw wooden planks on the clay soil under the yew tree. The coffin was lowered. The vicar said the words he had to say while Frances stared ahead of her, not down at the little coffin spattered now with ugly patches of mud, but through the holly hedge to the open field beyond where her father was running, pulled by the red kite with its snaky tail. She stood and watched, in her red wellingtons, with her coat fastened tightly across her chest. *See it fly! Watch it go! Looping, twisting, curling across the whole world!*

She felt a squeeze at her elbow. Tom, his face wet with tears, was staring at her veiled face.

'Shall we go? Do you want to stay?' his voice trembled.

'Poor Tom.' Those were the only words she spoke. She squeezed his hand; his shoulders heaved with spasms of sobs. She lowered her eyes for a fleeting glance. Gone. Freshly turned soil. Gone! Then, from deep inside herself, she felt a definite kick of life.

April 1987

Peta kicked the empty coke can along the pavement in front of her.

It would only take four minutes on a bike to get from home to the hospital. The bus took six minutes, but she had to allow up to forty minutes waiting as no reliable timetable seemed to exist. It used to take twenty minutes walking and that was only if she took the short cut over the field by the railway cutting. It was nearer thirty if she walked along the streets, but then the longer route took her from her mother's house past where her mother's best friend, Mollie and Peta's friend David lived, and past the house where her father Tom now lived with Annette. It was a pain, hoping not to be seen, dodging behind trees if a curtain twitched, flattening herself, so far as was possible, against garden fences and pretending to be invisible.

Still, her mother had made her swear not to take what she considered to be a dark and treacherous route but to stick to the well-lit streets, with neighbourhood watch stickers in the windows and bobbies on the beat . . . Frances never did understand that 'safe' meant something else to Peta.

And she had had a hard enough time persuading her mother that it was safe to work at the hospital in the first place.

'What do you want to do that for?'

''Cos I do.'

'What's wrong with the newspaper round?'

'I like reading to people . . . .'

That kind of comment was guaranteed to send her mother tight lipped.

'. . . Anyway, I thought *you'd* approve.'

Frances had flashed her an angry look. 'And what's that supposed to mean?'

'Nothing!' Peta had replied irritatingly.

Strangely enough, Frances apart – and there seemed to be nothing Peta did, or was, that Frances approved of – working at the hospital pleased everyone else. They called it 'community service' at school and even sanctioned it, and for the first time ever she was legitimately excused games on Wednesday afternoons.

Mavis and Lil, the two full-time nurses, thought she was great because she wasn't getting paid.

'That just proves I'm mad . . . no wonder I feel so at *home*,' Peta told them.

Janie was given specifically to Peta and told to do what she could. That was her problem. It was hard to know.

'What do you want Janie? What is it?'

Janie pointed with her finger, jabbing at the air.

'Janie! Janie! Janie!' she shouted.

'Come on. That's not good enough! Tell me what you want.'

Janie sat like a giant doll on the parquet floor, her legs stretched out stiffly in front of her, wearing white ankle socks and big brown sandals, a red gingham skirt and a white blouse with a little Peter Pan collar. Her hair, cropped like a helmet, had been cut square across her forehead. Her eyes squinted, her mouth opened and a thread of saliva fell from her lower lip and hung suspended.

Peta pulled a tissue out from her sleeve and caught the thread as it fell.

'Gotcha. Come on Janie. Try again!' But Janie had

descended into silence. She seemed to be staring with both eyes at the tip of her squat nose.

'Don't tell me . . .' Peta clapped a hand to her forehead with sudden realisation. '. . . *Not again!* Janie. Are you doing it? Janie? Yoo hoo!!' She waved a hand in front of Janie's eyes which gradually came apart and refocused on Peta's hand. Janie grinned.

'Janie, I could wallop you . . . or is that what you've been trying to tell me? I don't know. Come on then. Up!' Peta stood, legs apart, and held out her hands to Janie who grasped them tightly. 'One, two, three, up!'

She pulled Janie upright and hand in hand they walked through the recreation room, Janie's legs jerking from the hips. Peta led her into the little side-room which smelt of cabbage and disinfectant and old linoleum. Someone had stuck some pictures of Switzerland from an old calendar on the wall.

'Up on the bed.'

Janie looked at Peta. Her mouth started to open and shut and she made little grunting noises.

'I'm not lifting you up, mate!'

Janie was almost as tall as Peta, her shoulders thickset and her arms ironhard with muscle.

Sensing Peta's intransigence on this point, Janie crawled on to the bed and lay back docilely, pulling her red skirt up over her chest and opening her legs. She stared up at the cold Alpine peaks.

The nappy Peta took from the shelf behind her was as big as a towel. She folded it into a simple triangle and laid it on the bed, then pulling down the plastic pants she unpinned the yellowed napkin. Janie stared impassively at the Jungfrau while Peta cleaned her bottom quickly and sprinkled talc liberally over her before fastening the clean towel securely in place. She pulled the voluminous pants up over the nappy, patting Janie on the tummy.

'OK, you're done.'

'Oh, it's here you're hiding. What have you been up to, Janie? Giving her a hard time eh?' Lil wagged a finger at her.

'Yep,' said Peta, 'two in one afternoon.'

'It's all those prunes,' Lil told her. 'Come on Janie, time to go now. Nurse is here to take you back.'

Janie turned her head round slowly to stare at Lil.

'Come on love – sit up.' Peta took her hands again and pulled Janie into a sitting position, then stood her up and smoothed down her skirt.

Lil put her hand out. 'Come on, say goodbye to Peta. See her next week! Bye-bye Peta!'

Janie opened her mouth again, her tongue slipping forward and she gulped out a sound that could have been 'Bye'.

'Bye Janie! Be good.' Peta threw the soiled napkin into the bucket and washed her hands in the corner sink before walking through to the hall again. Jimmy, one of the old residents, a grey balaclava pulled well down over his face, was just wheeling the last of the chairs out.

'Bye Jimmy!' she called.

He turned and smiled when he heard her. 'Cheerio!'

Back in the office Peta filled the kettle, plugged it in and then automatically felt in her back pocket for her cigarettes. She had put one between her lips before she remembered: 'Damn it, no matches.' She'd have to wait for Lil or Mavis. She put a couple of tea bags into the pot and sat listening to the kettle.

Mavis was the first back. She flopped into a chair groaning. 'My oh my!'

'What's up with you?'

'I'm exhausted, that's what's up!' Mavis shook her head and wiped a hand over her forehead. 'My hair's soakin'. It's pourin' again.'

'Go curly if you're not careful.'

'Watchit cheeky!'

11

As Peta poured the water into the pot Mavis went on, 'All this rain! It gets you down. I feel right depressed.'

'Go back to Jamaica then,' suggested Peta, playfully.

'You! Watchit!!'

'Seriously Mave, I can't think why you ever left, all that sun and pineapples. *I* wouldn't have!'

'Not even to follow your own true love?'

'*Specially* not for that!!'

Mavis shook her head. 'I don't know about you Peta. You wait till you fall in love, then you'll see!'

'Huh. I'm not going to.'

'Oh, you say that now . . .'

'I've got too much sense!'

Peta didn't mind them really, always going on about boyfriends and falling in love. At least they came straight to the point, and she didn't mind them shaking their heads at her.

'What *can* you be talking about?' Lil asked, picking up the end of their conversation.

'Peta says she's got too much sense to get herself a boyfriend,' Mavis explained.

'No one would have me anyway,' said Peta without self-pity. 'I mean – look at me!!'

'Look all right to me!' Lil told her.

'Put your glasses back on!'

'You'd be all right if you'd wear something pretty,' Mavis told her. 'How come you never wear a dress?'

'Don't like 'em. Here, give us a light Lil.'

Lil, who was taking off her white coat, stopped and reached in her bag and threw a box of matches to Peta. She stood for a moment in her petticoat staring down at herself. 'Do you think I've lost anything?' She drew her breath in, squeezing her stomach muscles. The fat rolls were still visible against the silky pink slip.

'No,' said Peta.

'P'raps a little,' said Mavis more encouragingly.

Lil breathed out. 'God! I'm practically starving my-

12

self. No cakes! No potatoes!'

'You won't want any sugar then?' asked Peta.

'Just one, love.'

Peta smiled to herself as she passed the tea to them.

'You're a good girl underneath it all . . .' teased Lil, '. . . how's school?' she went on.

Peta made a face.

'Less said . . . eh?'

Peta nodded.

'Yes, well. You want to knuckle down and get those exams – you won't get to college without them.'

Mavis nodded her agreement. 'You can't do anything without exams these days.'

It was all right when they told her what to do. It seemed simple, but they knew life wasn't like that really. The routines they went over each time they sat together drinking tea were in some ways just a game. What was said was predictable, and comfortable. And it all made sense too, on one level, but that wasn't the level at which life is lived. Not really. And they all knew it.

Peta blew gently over her tea. 'Too hot for me – I don't know how you can drink it so boiling hot Lil.'

'Asbestos mouth, me,' Lil replied as she did every day.

'I still can't see why you need bloody exams to look after people like this!' Peta commented.

'Yes, well, that's life isn't it?' Lil too lit up a cigarette. 'I mean, there's no question you've got a gift with 'em, hasn't she Mave?'

'Oh yes. She's done wonders with Janie. When I think how that girl just used to sit and scream!'

'Well, I've got lots in common with 'em haven't I? Half way mental myself! . . .' Peta flicked ash into her saucer.

'Pah!' snorted Lil.

'. . . I've been an inmate after all,' Peta continued.

13

'What, here?!' Mavis stared at her.

'That weren't *you* . . . that were your mum!' corrected Lil.

'Well, that proves it's in the family!' Peta enjoyed playing this part of the script, pursuing her line doggedly, knowing that Lil would contradict her.

'Don't you listen to her, Mavis!'

'Took one look at me and decided life wasn't worth living.'

'Get away with you.'

'Bet you never felt like that when yours were born, did you?' questioned Peta.

'No, I just feels like that when I look at them now!' Mavis threw back her head and laughed loudly.

'Anyway, how is your mum?' asked Lil surreptitiously stirring another spoonful of sugar into her tea.

'She's sick of me . . . I know that!' It was what she *felt* but yet she knew that wasn't all of it.

'Oh, you're just saying that!' said Mavis firmly.

'It's true. At least . . . that's what she said.'

'She may have said it, doesn't mean to say it's true!' said Mavis, confident of being an authority on what mothers say to their children.

'You don't know my mum.'

'Well *I* do, and I'd say she was sick with worry my girl. And in my opinion you give her plenty of reason to be . . . you should take her feelings into account more.' Lil ended with a sniff. There was an uncomfortable pause.

Peta wasn't angry. She considered the justice of this advice. 'You're probably right,' she said, stubbing her cigarette out.

'Like I've said, you just want to get yourself a man,' Mavis told her emphatically. 'That'd keep you busy!'

Peta threw her a withering look.

'There's still time love,' Lil was agreeing with her colleague. 'Look at me . . . married at forty. I was

14

convinced that nobody would look twice at me but Reg don't mind looks, likes me fat too he says. Something to get his teeth into!' she chortled wickedly. 'You wait. Mr Right will come along one day.'

Peta snorted again and started to put on her ex-army jacket.

'You off now then?'

Peta nodded. 'See you next week.'

'Bye love. And go careful now,' said Mavis.

'Yes, and keep out of trouble.' Lil called after her.

It was no longer pouring but there was still a fine drizzle hanging in the evening air. She walked along the paths, past the low, dull red-brick buildings. The gardens themselves were beautiful, tended with care by some of the more active residents: tall colourful tulips, thick clumps of pink and white flocks; the main drive flanked with rose bushes. Peta was not surprised to see the usual group of inmates standing at the wire fence which overlooked the main road. Rain or shine, they stood staring out at the world beyond the limits of their safety.

The sound of a baby crying came drifting through the muffling damp. It came from the last ward block, set back and half screened by a ragged beech hedge. The cry rose in pitch and intensity with each step she took, filling her head with its pain and demand. When Peta passed the open doors the woman's scream came, a scream so piercing, so shocking, that it drowned the baby's crying.

April 1971

'Ssh! *Please* Mrs Piper, stop screaming.'

'That's not my baby!'

Nurse Frobisher stood, not knowing what to do. There had been nothing in the training! She tried again, leaning forward to offer the tiny baby, neatly parcelled in a white shawl.

'It is Mrs Piper. *It is.* Look, we put an identity tag on them the moment they're born. Honest.'

She even unwrapped one side of the shawl to point to the tiny bracelet, barely large enough to contain the information: Baby Piper. 6lb 10oz. 3:4:71.

Frances turned away and shut her eyes to retreat from it all, to fall back into that dark land. She wished she'd never bothered to climb. And such a long climb up, up and out to the light and the air it had been too. She couldn't find a way down into the dark dreamland again, try as she might. She shook her head impatiently on the white pillow. *Ruined! No way back now!*

'Leave me alone.' she moaned.

The nurse, inexperienced as she was, stood protectively holding the baby to her starched chest: 'Poor little thing. Doesn't your mummy want you eh? I'll have you.'

'Everything all right Nurse?' Sister called across to her, rather sharply. 'Come on now, no time to daydream.'

'Oh Sister, it's Mrs Piper. She won't take the baby. She says she's not hers!'

16

Sister stood still for a moment, unusual enough. 'Ah,' was her comment. 'Tell Mr Piper to come and speak to me when he returns will you?' she added.

'Don't be ridiculous Frances!' Tom's voice was heated. He ran his hand through his hair in exasperation. A bunch of flowers lay abandoned on the bed. 'They must know what they're doing. You're still drugged – upset.'

'I'm not drugged or upset. I *saw* my baby! He was red . . .'

'She,' he corrected quickly.

Frances ignored him. '. . . It was red, bloody, screwed up, ugly and had black hair sticking up all over its head. And eight hours later they bring me something golden with curls. A little doll! And they try to convince me that's mine! *I saw him.*'

He didn't try again. He patted her hand. 'I'll see what I can do love. I'll talk to someone.'

He did, but the sister's words were not quite as reassuring as he had hoped. Frances had been through a lot, sister agreed, it might be the drugs or a passing phase indeed, but the list of people to contact should the need for help arise filled Tom with foreboding.

'Now, I expect you'd like to see your daughter. She's a cracker.'

Tom lingered in the doorway.

'She wasn't like this with our son,' he fretted. 'But she did hope for another boy this time . . .'

'Well,' Sister conceded, 'that may well have something to do with it.'

'. . . Of course *I'm* delighted. *I* wanted a girl! he continued, smiling.

'Good,' she smiled more warmly back. 'I'm glad somebody's satisfied.'

17

April 1987

It was the kind of scream that stopped the blood — but only for a second before it broke into hysterical laughter. The swing doors of the ward block swung open and two male nurses frogmarched a tiny figure out of the building — the source of the scream.

'All right Ellie, that's enough. Quieten down now. *Calm down!*' — one of the nurses, in a voice that suggested this wasn't the first time this had happened.

'Shut it Ellie,' snapped the second nurse, more gruffly. 'You've done it again. I *told you* you wouldn't be able to stay if you got over-excited.'

Slowly Ellie realised what was happening as the words, and the sensation of the drizzle and the dark, gradually permeated her joy and excitement. Her voice quietened until, as she rounded the corner, her sobs died to whimpers and she slumped between the nurses like a rag doll.

Social club eh? So it was. Peta had forgotten. Five o'clock till seven, dancing and orange squash and a sing-song. Just look in. Why not? She unbuttoned her jacket and threw it over the back of the chair by the door . . .

'I'm going home tomorrow! Home tomorrow!!' Peta's hand was seized immediately and she was led in an ecstatic whirling dance by a woman in a yellow cardigan wrongly fastened, a short floral skirt and stout, clumpy shoes.

'Home tomorrow eh?' It probably wasn't true . . . but what the hell! She was happy and excited and why not? Suddenly Peta's hand was dropped and she was clutched round the waist, ballroom style. They stood face to face, waiting.

'Am I supposed to be the girl, or the boy?' Peta asked.

It must have been the funniest thing she'd ever said because her partner exploded in laughter, clapped one hand over her mouth and the other in her crotch, squeezing her knees together before she finally galloped away to the toilets.

Fred, the social organiser, in his home-knit Fair Isle pullover, rather short and baggy at the bottom, was getting a group together for community singing. Mr Arthur was ready at the piano. His repertoire, though rather limited, was played with feeling, the only drawback being that he always began when *he* was ready, not waiting for Fred's signal. By the time the inmates in the furthermost corners had joined in the singing, Mr Arthur had usually already launched into another song.

'*Daisy Daisy* . . .' It was an old favourite and sung with great gusto and much swaying from side to side.

Peta saw Gilbert sitting quietly by the window, staring as usual into a paper bag.

'It's empty Gilbert.'

'They've all gone,' he wailed.

'I expect you ate them.'

'No!'

She helped him to his feet, trying to draw him away from his sorrow and more into the circle of sound. He wouldn't sing but at least he bent his knees and rocked from side to side.

'Nice one, Gilbert,' Fred shouted encouragingly, winking in recognition at Peta.

But now Evelyn had also spotted her from across the room. Groaning inwardly, Peta wished her right hand had not been spare. It wasn't that Evelyn always clenched it so passionately, it was her simpering and pawing and lisping that made Peta want to get away.

'Hello!' Evelyn greeted her coyly. 'Hello Peta.'

'. . . *He drove the fastest milkcart in the west* . . .' sang Peta, one of the few who had heard the change of music.

'Hello,' Evelyn tried again, this time laying her head on Peta's shoulder.

'Hi Evelyn. Why don't you join in the singing?'

'Do you like my dress?' It was pink and frilly.

'Yes,' Peta lied.

'Do you think I'm pretty?'

'Yes. What about me? Do you think I'm pretty too?'

Evelyn didn't know how to answer that. She stood there blinking.

Gilbert had given up. He stood stranded in the middle of the hall hanging has head sadly.

'Come on Gilbert. I'll take you back now,' Peta promised, steering him back to his seat by the window. Evelyn followed them.

'Peta! Peta! Are you married?'

'No fear . . . I told you that last week.'

'Will you marry me?'

'The answer's still no, Evelyn. Sorry.'

Evelyn stood there, crestfallen, the corners of her mouth turned down, staring reproachfully at Peta, who was saved only by the arrival of the porters and nurses. One of the sisters, a dark cape thrown over her uniform, her hair still glistening with rain, came to take Evelyn away.

'Well now, Evelyn. Has she turned you down again?' she winked at Peta. Evelyn nodded. 'Still playing hard to get, eh?'

Peta smiled. 'Bye Evelyn.' But Evelyn was too wounded to reply.

In her inside pocket she had one, she was sure. Yes. Covered with fluff! She wiped it on her sleeve. 'Here you are Gilbert. Toffee.'

His eyes lit up with great joy. 'Toffee!' he repeated, turning it over in his hands like a precious jewel.

'Come on Gilbert. You'll miss the bus,' a nurse called over to him.

Peta buttoned up her jacket and was on the point of leaving when Fred came over to her. 'Thanks,' he said earnestly. 'Much appreciated.'

'I like it here, it's my second home,' she told him lightly. 'I can handle it. At least nothing's complicated.'

April 1971

'Wake up Mrs Piper. Here's someone calling for you. Come on, sit up.'

Sister was handling it all now. She held the baby expertly in one arm; with the other she plumped the pillows and helped Frances to half-sit.

'There we are dear. Hold her firmly now.' She had positioned France's arm into a crook, and quickly placed the baby in it before Frances could move.

'I feel cold,' Frances announced suddenly.

'Cold dear? I'll get you a cardy, shall I?'

'No – inside – *cold!*'

'Don't you worry about that, my dear. It often happens. It's all your hormones settling down,' Sister told her, confident. 'They'll sort themselves out in a day or two. Mrs Gibbs . . . Mrs Gibbs! Come over here a moment. she called to the woman in the bed opposite, still huge under her candlewick dressing gown.

Mrs Gibbs waddled over, placing her feet, in their pink feathery mules, rather wide apart.

'Look at this. Something to encourage you dear.'

A smile of natural delight spread over Mrs Gibbs' face. 'Oh how cute . . . just look at her. Isn't she gorgeous! It is a she, isn't it?'

'Yes,' chipped in Sister quickly. 'A *perfect* little girl.'

'Oh I do hope mine's a girl . . . no well, I don't mind that much . . . as long as it's got the right number of everything, that's the main worry. But Don, that's my husband, I think he wants a girl. Well, they're more fun aren't they? Ah, look at her . . . Bless her! *Look* at her little hands!' She held out a finger and the baby gripped her tightly.

Mollie Gibbs sat on the bed, still leaning over the baby. 'My first you know. I'm terrified,' she confessed to Frances. 'Go on . . . tell us. What's it like?'

'Hell,' said Frances shortly.

'Oh.'

'Don't you listen, Mrs Gibbs. You'll love it,' Sister said in a jocular tone.

When Nurse Frobisher shook Frances awake, she sat up abruptly. Mollie Gibbs was back in her bed opposite, the sheet pulled up to her chin, her face white but restful.

'What did she have?' Frances asked.

'Mrs Gibbs? A little boy. David she's calling him, and he's just fine. Cup of tea?'

'Thank you.'

'Sugar?'

'No thanks.'

'I'll give you time to get that down before I bring the little horror.' Nurse Frobisher smiled as she straightened the already neat covers. 'What are you going to call her? Got any names lined up yet?' she asked conversationally, checking the chart hooked over the end of France's bed.

'Peta.' Frances sipped the iron liquid.

Nurse Frobisher looked surprised.

'Peter?' she repeated.

'Yes.'

'Oh. With an 'a'. Well, it's unusual anyway. Different. Peta . . .' she tried the sound again, '. . . Yes, it's growing on me.'

'No, Fanny. *Please*.' Tom had hold of her hand.

'It's what I want,' she told him stubbornly.

23

'Well, she's mine too!' he reminded her petulantly.

'You said I could choose. You said you'd leave it to me, that you didn't mind,' she retorted hotly.

'I know . . . I know . . . but . . .' he sighed and sat back glumly. He'd liked it the first time round, though even then it had taken time before he was certain. Her idea of course – Peter Piper.

'It's a must,' she had told him. He remembered her laughing and laughing, 'My little Peter Piper. Peter Piper!' He remembered her teaching him the tongue twister too; it became his name: Peterpiper. Anyway, she asked, how could Tom object when *his* parents had called *their* sons Tom and Jerry? Ah, but that wasn't *deliberate*, he had told her.

'Well, *I'm* not calling her *that*,' Nance said decisively when she visited Frances that evening. Her daughter flashed her a hostile look.

'Tom's agreed,' she told her quickly.

Tom shrugged his shoulders helplessly.

'It's nonsense,' Nance continued. 'Here . . . let me hold her, love.'

The baby was relinquished without fuss.

Nance held Peta next to her face. Soft new skin against soft old skin. 'Little darling,' she crooned. 'Soft as a petal. That's what I'll call her. Petal. And if that's a problem, I'll just call her Pet.'

24

May 1987

'Petal . . . Petal! Oh my God. What's happened to you?'

Nance had opened her front door tentatively at first. Something had woken her, perhaps something falling, something from outside but she didn't know what it could be. Deep asleep she'd been, and woken to find the television still on, flickering a coloured light-show across her quilt. Oliver, her sober middle aged cat dedicated to his own comforts, was curled inside the curve of her body. He too had heard something, his head now held taut, his eyes wide.

Then came the moan, the long, low despairing moan, from the porch outside. Nance had jumped up; no fear, just responding to pain. Oliver, terrified, slipped past her into the night as she opened the door.

Nance hadn't thought of Peta but she knew immediately it was her. She bent down, frail as she was, clasping the leather-coated figure to her. Peta scrabbled over the red-tiled porch, pulling herself nearer, into a smaller, rounder shape and rocked against her grandmother, letting the tears wash down her face.

'I can't lift you my pet,' her grandmother was sobbing too. 'You're just too big for poor old Nance. Can you get on your feet my poor darling? Come inside. We can't be staying here all night . . . whatever would Mr Jenkins say when he brought the milk?!'

In spite of everything, Peta started giggling, and then her giggles turned to laughter, deep raucous laughter that almost tipped over into sobbing again. She picked herself and her rucksack up and, still laughing, followed her grandmother into the cottage and crashed down into one of the easy chairs.

'Everything's shrunk,' she protested. 'It's all shrunk!'

'I won't say it . . .' answered Nance as she struggled to heave off Peta's great leather boots.

'My God child! Look at these filthy socks!'

Peta stared miserably down at her feet, her big toes sticking clear out from the worn socks which smelt rancid and bad.

'Oh Nance,' she started wailing again. 'I'm disgusting, *I'm disgusting!*'

'You're my Petal. You're as lovely as ever. It's just the socks . . .' Nance replied in a matter of fact tone as she carried the socks out to the kitchen and threw them into the rubbish bin.

'Let's burn the lot!' Peta shouted after her.

'Good idea. We'll have a bonfire tomorrow, if the wind's in the right direction and not blowing straight into the Masseys' kitchen. Like we used to in the old times . . . do you remember, Pet? . . . That bonfire we had . . .'

'When the pine trees caught fire . . .'

'. . . and the hose wouldn't reach . . .'

'. . . and those buckets were so heavy . . .'

'. . . You were smaller then . . .'

'. . . and Mr Massey came tearing up the hill with his water pump!'

'. . . and I had that fire extinguisher just sitting in the hall all the time. I never even thought of it!'

The recollection gave them both the space and the time they needed; they could begin to relax now and be practical and unemotional.

Peta undressed, and sat in Nance's quilted dressing gown while Nance bathed the cut on her face.

'I think you should have a stitch,' she said doubtfully.

26

'It's gaping rather. You'll have a nasty scar,' she went on as Peta began to shake her head.

'Nothing much to disfigure,' she said without self-pity. 'Oh, I'm too tired. I just want to go to bed, Nance.' The whisky was wearing off now, leaving her with a metallic taste in her mouth and a leaden head.

'Not until you've had a bath and washed that hair my girl,' her grandmother told her firmly.

'Oh Nance . . .' Peta started, but surrendered the protest with some kind of relief.

It *had* all shrunk somehow. Used to be really high, that bath. Couldn't see over the side; she'd had to climb up on the cork-topped footstool with the china potty inside. Where had that got to? Shorter too; now she couldn't stretch out anymore. Felt different, somehow. Used to feel all gritty on the bottom.

Tap tap. Nance entered with a towel, averting her eyes. So much steam. No need. Anyway, what's this in the bath?

'A mat?!'

'To stop me slipping!'

'It's like sitting on an octopus!'

'Oh Petal,' Nance laughed. 'You've got it the wrong way up! Oooh! And just look at your poor head! Let me bathe it.'

She did, with her real sponge, gently. Warm on Peta's temple, drawing up the throbbing, all that pain, dissolving it into warmth and liquid. And Peta lay, eyes closing, hair floating round her shoulders like seaweed. That's better.

'Nance . . .'

'Um . . .'

'Do you love me?'

They both knew each other too well.

'What do you want?'

'A fag.'

'*Petal!* How could you! In the bath!!'

27

'I know. I know. It's disgusting . . . *I'm* disgusting. You hate smoke. *I* hate myself! *Please* . . . in my jacket,' she called after Nance.

In warm water things dissolve: time, pain, motion, misery. With her eyes closed and a warm flannel covering her face, rising and falling against her lips, Peta was able to let memories wash round her: Janie, the hospital, other comfortable things.

It wasn't all bad. Look on the bright side she told herself, with forced lightness, though she didn't feel light. Heavy, like a dead weight and she needed to take a huge lungful of air, to rise over it. She exhaled the air in a long, slow sigh. There was Mavis and Lil – they liked her – it was possible then. She could listen to them and hear what they were saying. Then there was Janie. That near-smile made her feel good when she remembered it. There was no problem there. It was always coming out into the crazy world that made her feel angry, confused, impatient with what she saw as a conspiracy to make things difficult.

The only way was to pretend nothing hurt, nothing affected her. It was hard enough convincing the rest of the world, but to convince herself was an impossible task. Underneath the flannel, Peta frowned in pain. Mike, the accident, the mess with Frances. Running away was no answer, she knew, but the inside felt so different from the outside, the big girl with the broad shoulders and the big boots! Peta shook her head and screwed up her eyes. She parted her lips and sucked the flannel in and sucked on the warm moisture.

Bugger, bugger, bugger them all! Peta rolled her head from side to side against the hard porcelain of the bath. The water slapped against the narrow sides, rising higher and higher until a final roll sent a wave into the air to land with a distant splat on the linoleum floor.

'Oh Nance, help me, please help me,' she moaned.

The flannel had grown chill and when Peta peeled it away from her face, the stain of her blood on it was watery and brown.

Nance tapped at the door a second time and waited a discreet moment before opening it. Peta made no attempt to move.

'Here! And don't ask me to do anything else! I'll put it over on the chair.'

'But I can't reach,' Peta protested, putting out her hand helplessly. 'Don't make me get out!'

With a laugh Nance passed her the saucer with the one cigarette and the box of matches. 'Just don't ask me to light it Peta. There I do draw the line. Neither am I going to stand here and watch you smoke it. Some things are better done behind closed doors!'

'True.' acknowledged Peta, flicking the water off her fingers and putting the cigarette between her lips.

May 1971

'*What* a crush!' Nance sank panting into a chair, depositing her laden shopping bags on the table.

'Did you get my cigarettes, Mum?'

Nance nodded and sat slumped, hand on her chest, as Frances searched through the first bag: cauliflower, Lux Flakes, tins of soup.

'Not in this one,' she said, vexed, and started on the next: disposable nappies, cotton buds, Milton, evaporated milk, sugar, cereal.

'Nor this one. *Mum!*' she yelled.

'Hang on. Let me catch my breath . . .' Nance's bosom heaved up and down, '. . . you're smoking too much my girl!' she added grimly.

'*Did* you get them?'

'Yes. Yes. Look, in my pocket all the time.' She tossed the packet to Frances, who caught it and swiftly ripped off the cellophane. Placing a long cigarette between her lips, she inhaled deeply.

'That's better!'

Her mother sniffed in disgust and took her scarf from round her neck, wafting the blue smoke away with it.

'How's she been?' she asked.

'Awful. Screamed her head off. I just put her in her cot and closed the door on her,' Frances replied, taking another long pull on her cigarette and brushing flecks of ash from her peach-silk dressing gown.

'Poor little mite. Must be something wrong . . . she doesn't cry for nothing, you know.'

'Huh!'

'P'raps she's hungry.'

'She's *never* satisfied! One big mouth. Screams until she's fed; screams until she's asleep; screams until she's fed again.' Frances picked up an emery board from the side and started filing her nails.

'Oh, I hate that noise,' Nance shuddered.

'Won't be a minute.'

'Make us a cuppa, love,' Nance asked, stretching her legs out in front of her and starting to massage her swollen knee joints.

'I'm getting old . . . that's the truth of the matter. I can't cope with town. Such a crush in the shops. Queues too. I'm not used to it Frances. At least in the village we don't have to queue. If there's someone else in the shop Mrs Hodge lets me sit behind the counter,' she laughed.

Frances switched on the kettle and spooned instant coffee into two cups.

Nance sniffed. 'Funny cuppa!'

'Sorry. Wasn't thinking.'

Something in the tone of her voice made Nance look at her sharply. 'Frances, are you feeling all right? Look at me.'

Frances stared unflinchingly into her mother's pale eyes and said nothing.

'I wish you'd tell me,' Nance pleaded.

The baby started crying. Frances slammed her cup down. Anger flushed her cheeks pink. 'Not again!'

'Leave her. *Relax*. I'll go.' Nance struggled to her feet, but Frances had already gone, racing up the stairs then flinging open a door.

'What's the matter now?' she demanded and downstairs Nance caught the trembling note in her daughter's voice and sank back into her chair wearily.

'Don't interfere, Nancy!' she told herself firmly, taking a sip of her coffee, her face wrinkling with distaste.

31

Frances soon returned to the kitchen with the baby – thrown over her shoulder like a cardigan – who stared at the world moving past her through ink-blue eyes.

'Well, Petal. What was all that about eh?' The baby stared blankly at her grandmother, dribbling down the back of Frances' silk dressing gown.

Nance stretched her arms out, 'Here, let me take her.'

Frances handed her over, quickly. 'I'll make up a bottle!'

'Given up then love?'

'It's easier to see how much she's getting, and anyway Tom can feed her this way too.' Frances was defensive and brusque.

Keeping her thoughts to herself, Nance cupped the baby's head in her hand and crooned softly to her. 'There's my little Petal. *Little Pet*. Had a pain did you . . . a pain in your little tummy?'

'*God* mother! Why do people talk to babies as though they're mentally defective? Why do people talk to babies full stop!'

Nance ignored her. 'What are you staring at, eh? I think it's my brooch. Look Frances . . . look at her! She's seen my brooch!!'

Frances was spooning powdered milk into a bottle. She looked up, and smiled suddenly. Then the doorbell rang sharply, and she dropped the spoon.

'Damn it!' she cried, grabbing Peta. 'You go. I can't go to the door like this . . . *Oh don't you start!!*' The baby's face puckered as she shuddered into a loud wail of protest.

'You took her from me too quickly. You've frightened her!' Nance said. Still in her hat and coat, she went to the front door.

'Oh hello Mollie love. Come in, come in.'

'Hello Nance. Hope it's not inconvenient. Are you just off somewhere?'

'No. *No!*'

Mollie manoeuvred her huge carriage pram into the hallway. 'You need a licence with these! Don says he's going to put 'L' plates on,' she giggled.

Nance peered into the pram, 'And how is little David? I can't see him . . . where's he gone?!'

Mollie's face clouded for an instant. 'Oh don't tease Nance . . . he slips down under the blankets. Don says I ought to fill the rest of the pram with a pillow!'

'Oh, he's full of ideas.'

'Yes,' Mollie answered proudly, and still looking at her baby, she went on, 'You know I keep thinking he's dead . . . I keep checking in the night!' She flushed suddenly, realising what she'd said. 'Oh Nance, I'm so sorry . . .'

'No no, don't be. I remember doing just the same myself with Frances. Hark at her now!'

Real, quavering screams came from the kitchen, rising and trembling then falling. 'Please be quiet, *please be quiet*,' Frances was pleading with Peta.

'Here, I'll have a go.' Nance took hold of her and walked away, crooning soothingly. 'Now, now, little Petal . . . shhhh . . . shhhh!

'I'm sorry Mollie . . .'

Mollie noted that Frances' eyes were full of tears.

'Oh it's OK, honestly. I know how you feel. I get to the end of my rope sometimes too. Mind you, he's a good boy, doesn't give me much trouble. Touch wood.' She tapped the table top.

'That's formica!'

'Oh.' Mollie looked around for a moment, then laughed at herself. 'Don's being a brick, a real brick!'

'You're lucky there,' Frances told her. 'Tom's so ham-fisted . . . nervous I guess. I'd almost rather he didn't try.'

'Oh well, I can sympathise. I get ever so nervous myself. Frances,' Mollie paused as though about to say something very significant, 'have you ever dropped her?'

Frances laughed. 'No. Not even deliberately.'

'Oh, it wasn't deliberate!' Mollie protested wide-eyed. 'I daren't tell Don.'

Frances threw back her head and roared with laughter. 'Did you really? *Really?* Drop him?!'

Mollie nodded seriously. 'It wasn't funny. I didn't laugh, I can assure you.'

Nance stayed with her daughter for a further fortnight but finally decided she must return to the village. After all there were the budgies to think of and Mrs Hodge – she couldn't put upon her indefinitely. And poor Mr Standwick – who was going to change his library books for him? Jeremy Tudor could be relied on to come in and feed the cat, if only just to get out of his mum's way, but of course the real reason she decided to leave, which she never admitted to, was that she was simply exhausted.

Peta was a poor sleeper, true, and Nance had spent many hours of darkness listening to her piercing screams of protest. But it wasn't that so much as the tension. She hadn't been like that, Frances, with her last one. There was something wrong, but somehow Nance didn't seem able to help. Frances had taken to shouting at her too, and *that* Nance could do without! Of course Frances admitted she was under strain, and knew she was getting on Nance's nerves. Perhaps she *would* be better off on her own; settle down, get into a routine. So Nance left, leaving her number with Mollie . . . just in case. Nice girl, Mollie.

Back to her cottage then, with its country quiet and deep peace, its outside smells of earth and cows and wind and full-headed roses and its inside smells of lavender and cats, old wood and sweetness.

May 1987

Laying on her side under the heavy quilt, knees tucked under her chin, Nance's winceyette nightie crept cosily round her, smelling of linen cupboards and talcum powder and sweetness.

Nance bent to kiss Peta.

'When I look at you snuggled there just as you used to, I want to sing you a nursery rhyme.'

'Feel free,' Peta mumbled.

'And then I bend close and I get a whiff of stale whisky and smoke!' she laughed.

'And toothpaste!'

'Well . . .' Nance conceded, '. . . *and* toothpaste,' sitting herself on the edge of the bed, just beneath where Peta's knees were bent and patted Peta's hair anxiously.

'Still damp. You'll wake with a cold!'

'Don't fuss.'

Nance sighed. 'Stopped bleeding,' she observed.

There was a pause. Peta didn't open her eyes and at first Nance thought she had drifted into sleep.

'Did you love Frances?' Peta asked suddenly.

Nance was not prepared for that question. 'Well now, what a funny thing to ask! You mean do I?'

'No, I mean *did* you. When she was first born?'

'I did. I did.'

'That's how it should be . . . mothers and babies.'

'Yes of course. That's the way of it.'

Peta had to go on now, and frame the questions which had never been shaped into words before. It was safe and warm and snug and far away from it all here and Nance just might know. She might be able to tell her something.

'I wonder why Frances didn't love me then.'

There was no self-pity or self-mockery in Peta's voice so Nance did not protest.

'Well. It *was* difficult. She did I'm sure of it, underneath. She does . . .' she went on, ignoring Peta's tiny snort, '. . . but, oh I don't know, Peta. I really don't know why. It was just easier for me. I'm a lucky one.'

It was difficult for Peta to consider someone so remote from her, known only by his indistinct photograph in a frame; and a small marble headstone. Even when the thoughts had come into her head, she found the words almost impossible to say.

'It was my brother wasn't it?' she said quietly.

'Not him!' Nance shook her head emphatically. 'Not him . . . poor wee mite. But maybe him *and* her: something between them, a space inside her which she thought you could fill.'

'But I was the wrong shape!' Peta said, not as a joke this time but seriously, and she sighed just once curling her knees up more tightly. 'I think I'll go to sleep now. I like sleep.'

Nance smiled. 'I know.'

May 1971

'Do you love him?' Frances asked suddenly. Their two babies were laying naked and squirming on a towel by the fireside.

Mollie looked up in amazement. 'David?! *The baby?*'

Frances nodded and pulled thoughtfully on her cigarette.

'Of course I do!' Mollie leant forward and touched his tummy with her lips.

'It's unthinkable not to, isn't it?' Frances pursued.

'Well, it's not natural, is it?' Mollie said, sensibly.

'Well,' Frances sighed. 'I'm unnatural then. I don't love her. I don't. I just don't feel anything.'

Mollie looked at her blankly at first and then with horror. 'Don't say that, you don't mean it.'

'But I do. I do!'

To Mollie's concern, Frances suddenly crumpled. Her china mask cracked and tears welled out and drenched her cheeks. Mollie put her arms clumsily round her and rocked her to and fro.

'Don't cry, Frances! Don't cry. You're worn out. That's what makes you feel this way.'

'How can I love something that screams at me all day long . . . it's so unlovable!' Frances wailed miserably.

'Ssh! Don't cry. I know you love her really. You just *think* you don't. You'll be OK if you get some sleep. Go to bed. I'll look after the pair of them this afternoon. I'm lucky: David's so good.'

'I won't be able to sleep,' moaned Frances.

'Nonsense, I'll bring you some cocoa . . .'

Frances shook her head wearily.

'Well, I'd go and see the doctor. He'll give you something. He'll help,' Mollie added with confidence. Then, tentatively, 'Have you talked to Tom about it?' she asked.

'No we don't seem to be able to talk any more,' Frances confessed sadly.

'Well you should, you know. Tell him how you feel. He can't know if you don't tell him! I'm sure it would help. Don's been a tower of strength to me.'

Frances stopped crying. She stayed with her head resting on Mollie's shoulder for a moment longer then sat up suddenly and resolutely. 'I'll got to the doctor. Yes, I'll tell him everything. Could you look after Peta? Could you?' Her eyes were animated for the first time since Mollie had met her. Frances leant forward and kissed her on the forehead.

Mollie flushed, rather taken aback. 'Go on! Quick. You'll just catch the surgery.'

Frances glanced quickly at her reflection in the mirror over the fireplace. 'My God! I can't go like this. Where's my make-up?'

And Mollie watched her as she creamed her pale face into a uniform golden tan, carefully applied her lipstick, and combed her honey-coloured hair into place.

Frances smelled the beer on Tom's breath as he kissed her. She turned away in anger.

'Stopped off at the pub?' she asked coldly.

'Only a quickie!' he confessed guiltily. He needed a drink after a day with the turbo-engines . . . Frances just didn't understand.

'You could have been home helping me,' she rebuked him petulantly.

'Don't nag,' he replied. 'Jerry's invited us round for Sunday lunch,' he added cheerfully.

She nodded.

'Well, say something.'

'Fine. What do you want me to say?' She turned away quickly.

He sighed. 'Drink?'

She shook her head and he went quickly to the sideboard and poured himself a generous whisky. Frances clumped about noisily in the kitchen while he hovered uneasily at the door.

'Mollie been round?'

'Yes.'

'Where's the paper?' He wandered back to the sitting room.

'Haven't seen it.'

He collected it from the letter box and settled himself in an easy chair. From upstairs he heard the baby cry and he shifted uncomfortably in his chair. When the cries grew stronger, he called out, 'Baby's crying.'

'Oh,' Frances replied pointedly.

'Shall I get her?'

'If it won't disturb your reading!'

'Frances! Don't be like this,' he pleaded, draining his whisky which burned the back of his throat. Upstairs he pulled back the covers of his daughter's cot and a sharp smell of ammonia hit him.

'Come on, Peta,' he said softly. 'Don't cry.' Slipping off his suit jacket, he went through to the bedroom and collected a towel from the linen cupboard.

'What are you doing?' Frances called.

'Coming.'

He threw the towel over his shirt for protection, and picking up his hot and screaming infant he patted her back gently. Her sobs gratifyingly changed to hiccups. Downstairs he snapped on the radio and began to dance Peta round the room to the disco beat.

Frances stood in the doorway. '*What do you look like!*'

He looked up anxiously but was relieved to see

Frances smile. He wiggled his hips provocatively in time to the music and danced over to her and took her hand; 'Care to dance?'

'No,' she laughed and pulled free. 'What's my towel doing?'

'Nothing much.'

'Why is my towel over your shoulder Tom?'

'Because I didn't want to soak my best suit.'

'You wouldn't think of changing her I don't suppose!' Frances was cold again and Tom sighed and turned the music off. He laid Peta down on the changing mat and her little face started to pucker again alarmingly.

'No,' he implored as he removed the sodden nappy. It was warm and heavy. He took a clean one from the box, unfolded it, and, lifting the baby up by her feet, slid it under her bottom. He tried to ease on the sticky tapes but his fingers were unsteady. Peta was so tiny it made him nervous. Wherever he stuck the tape, it was wrong somehow: too far to the left, too far to the right; and then if he tried to move it, the tape lost its stickiness.

'Too loose!' As soon as he held her up, it seemed to fall; he tugged at it with his free hand and as he did so Peta's head lolled dangerously.

'It's coming off already!' Frances observed, with contempt in her voice.

'I can't seem to get them tight,' he apologised.

'Give her to me . . . . I'll feed her!'

'I could if you like,' he offered meekly.

'No, *I'll* do it. You only give her wind.'

It seemed so unfair, but better let it pass, he told himself as he replenished his empty glass and settled back with his paper.

'I must talk to you Tom.' The pressure on his shoulder told him he must have nodded off.

He snapped awake. There was something about the intensity in her voice which banished his drowsiness immediately. Frances sat very straight, perched on the edge of the sofa. She was wearing her peachy dressing gown with the lace collar that he'd bought for her after Peter had died. She wore no make-up and her face was pale. He noticed two dark circles under her eyes, as though she'd been bruised.

'I feel very cold towards the baby. I don't love her,' she said clearly.

'Don't say that . . .'

'It's the truth! *Let me say it!*' Her voice rose.

'All right. All right . . . you're tired.'

'I'm more than tired.'

'I'm trying to help! But you criticise me so . . .' his voice trailed off.

'I went to the doctor today.'

'And what did he say?' he asked hopefully.

'Not to fuss, basically.'

'Oh.'

'He told me to discuss it with you.'

'Well, what am I supposed to say?'

'I don't know. *I don't know!*' Frances stood up trembling. She walked to the window, turning her back on him. The curtains were not yet drawn and a cold shaft of moonlight fell on her face. 'All I know is that someone's got to do something!'

May 1987

It was one of those nights which seemed so long that Peta felt as though she'd fallen through the darkness into another experience of time altogether.

She woke with the moonlight cutting across her face. She hadn't expected to wake into anything except the usual colour, but everything now was metallic shades of silver and lead and mercury, clear and cold.

The outlines of the furniture were sharp: the bed end, the wardrobe, the chest of drawers with its bright mirror, the old chest beneath the window; the dark beams arched over her like a giant rib-cage. The curtains hadn't been drawn quite together. She turned lazily but it was only pretending; she *knew* she wouldn't be able to ignore that light, even on her back.

Taking a deep breath she threw back the covers and padded to the window. It was cold, deliciously cold and instead of racing quickly back to the warmth, she rested her forehead on the smooth window-pane. Her hair felt warm and damp. If she knelt on the chest and pulled back the curtains, she could see the clear horizon of the hills and a few spindle silhouettes of trees against the sky. How black they seemed until you looked at the blackness beneath them, the earth which swallowed up all detail. And there was the blackness above the night sky, clear now, with rain clouds pulled away by the wind.

Peta breathed deeply and felt the night air filling her chest. As she did so, she lifted her eyes away from the ground and the earth to the black dome over her head. Stars! There were millions of them, light years away, shivering, like candle flames, yet in no danger of being extinguished . . . pinpricks in a dark cloth.

The moon was high too, not quite full, one cheek shaved off its final crescent: a pale moon, with a sad and weighty face. As Peta stared at it, it was as though she was looking into a strange mirror of light. But she didn't like to look for long . . . it made her feel uncomfortable somehow, X-rayed, as though the light was penetrating secret concerns.

With something like irritation she turned her back on that moon face, jumped into bed, turned away from the light and fell instantly into a deep sleep.

June 1971

Gradually Frances recovered, recovered enough to realise that she wanted to go home and carry on. Recovered enough, too, to realise what she would have to do and say for the hospital to release her. But the difference in her was also true; it wasn't something you could pretend after all. Things weren't quite right yet, this she knew, but they *were* getting better, she was going in the right direction. At least she had accepted little Peta now. She did feel for Peta, when she cried Frances wanted to feed her or hold her, not throw her across the room.

It had all become better from the time when she had begun to see a resemblance, to see *his* face emerging in Peta's. It was that which made it all seem possible now. Then she was discharged, and when Tom collected her, he was shaking with what he said was excitement. There was a vase of tulips on the dining-room table and a shepherd's pie in the oven. The house was very clean and very empty. It was as though nobody really believed it – believed that anything Had happened at all.

Frances held out against her mother's invitation for longer than Nance expected. She was depressed of course, at needing to go away again so soon. She had hoped that things would be easier at home though Mollie's company and friendship was one source of uncomplicated pleasure: they shopped together, changed library books and sat in each other's houses,

44

drank coffee and exchanged gossip. Mollie's Don made Frances uneasy, however. He was nervous in her company and deliberately wary of his wife's crazy friend, as Frances was certain he thought of her as being.

Each day she seemed to need to escape more urgently, and from Tom particularly. If she could just get away from him for a bit, perhaps everything would become clearer. Of course Tom acted the Hurt Husband but secretly he was relieved. It wasn't the baby, in spite of the broken nights and the endless feeding and changing, the dried sick and dribble on his office suits. It was Frances, frozen Frances, who made him feel like an intruder in his own home, and unwelcome in her life.

Nance's cottage could have no memories of childhood days for Frances. Nance had decided, when her husband died and Frances had married, that at last she could make her own private dream come true.

She had bought this little cottage complete with rambling rose, water-butt and leaden window-panes. Mornings she spent in the wilderness, as she called it, with her secateurs, cutting back the couch grass and the columbine, fashioning little flower beds, preparing soil, planting, and building rockeries. Afternoons she spent inside, ripping up old linoleum, tearing layers of paper away from the walls, stripping off old paint until she found the original shell. Lovingly she had replastered and repainted the walls in bright clean shades, exposed the old beams and blackened the fire grates. She'd made chintzy covers for her old settee and armchair, put down rosy carpets and placed china ornaments on the mantelpiece. Fussy, Frances called it but Nance replied simply, 'It's how I like it.' Her final touch was the bird cage with its two budgies, and the kitten that Mr Massey from the farm next door had given her.

'I love my little home!' she would affirm out loud almost every day and she confessed it again to Frances as she led her up the tiny winding staircase now.

'Mind your head on that beam love!' she warned. Frances ducked on to all fours.

There was one little room upstairs, snug beneath the eaves and Frances knew her mother never slept there herself even when alone. She had a bed in the living room.

'Can't manage these stairs at night,' she'd explained; 'and the waterworks aren't what they used to be!'

The room was spotless. There was a paper of blue roses on the walls and curtains of blue and white gingham at the windows. 'Guess where I got that material?' asked Nance as she stood catching her breath, one hand on the dressing table for support.

'Give up.'

'Your old school summer dress!' Nance chortled.

'*Mother!* You can't mean it,' Frances took hold of the material in disbelief.

'Got a cot too . . . borrowed it from Mrs Massey's niece in the next village.' She proudly patted the side. The cot was old, and the paint chipped. There was a transfer of a lamb stuck on the end at rather an odd angle. Nance pointed to the quilt inside. 'And I've just made that for her too!'

It was beautiful. Ice pink and dizzy with frills and flounces. 'Pink for a little girl. Pink for my Petal,' she announced clearly.

Frances smiled down at it. 'I hope I don't fall down those stairs with her,' she retaliated.

'Don't say so!' Nance was horrified. 'They *are* a bit steep,' she agreed, concerned.

'Oh I don't think I will; just a thought. Look at this view!' Frances pushed open half of the window and stuck out her head. There were cows right underneath her and she could see the fields stretching away left and right, to the hills that bumped along the horizon. Nothing but green grass, trees, cows and black crows.

She knew it was good. It was good to be here. Perhaps, after all, this *was* what she needed.

Nance, puffing and panting, pushed open the door and stood in disbelief. There was Peta, poor wee mite, screaming, her face purple with the veins raised and throbbing in her neck; and there was Frances sleeping through it all! Admittedly she was tossing her head from side to side and moaning a bit, but when Nance lifted the baby out of the cot, Frances turned over with a deep sigh, pulling the covers over her head.

'You're soaked through! My poor darling,' Nance said, hugging Peta tightly. 'Now, hold on to your Nance, my love, for the stairs. You be my baby monkey, Pet . . . cling on. If only I'd thought, I'd have put you downstairs with me,' she added grimly.

'But what would you have had to say about that, eh?' she asked Oliver, who wound himself through her legs as she stood in the kitchen, studiously ignoring the baby Nance was holding.

'I know, I know! You're hungry too . . . but you'll just have to take second place,' she told the cat as she reached for the Ostermilk.

Outrageous! Oliver sat down quickly to attend to an irritation near his tail.

Peta, pacified by the movement now, waited patiently while Nance, somewhat slowly and inefficiently, made up a bottle and mixed the breakfast gruel.

'Looks like Polyfilla!' She sniffed. 'Doesn't smell unlike either. Come on then; let's be having you.'

They sat cuddled together in a cosy chintz armchair, Oliver watching disdainfully from the kitchen doorway, his nose twitching at the distasteful odours of milk and ammonia. Then Nance bathed her in the washing-up bowl, talced and changed her and dressed her too with clothes from the suitcase which Frances had neglected to take upstairs.

She'd also fed Oliver and was engrossed in burying her face into the baby's neck and making her laugh when Frances finally appeared, her hair dishevelled and her face still heavy, and with a faraway feel about her. 'Whatsatime?' she asked.

Oh . . . you have slept well my darling . . . it's half past ten. Oh, that's the medicine for you, country air. Few nights of that and we'll have you right as rain, won't we?' She repeated to Peta: 'Won't we?'

Frances yawned loudly and moved across to the kitchen.

'Here love, I'll make a nice cup of tea . . . take the baby,' Nance called after her.

'It's all right.'

Nance settled back but uneasily.

When Frances reappeared she had a cigarette in her hand and was blowing smoke rings into the air. Nance managed to bite her tongue.

'I thought I'd just run up to Mrs Hodge and get a few things for lunch from the shop. We need bread, and I think the fresh air would do Peta good.' She couldn't resist that much.

Frances brushed aside the comment, along with ash from her nightdress. 'OK.'

'Anything I can get you?' Nance offered and then regretted it.

'Just some cigarettes, if that doesn't go against your principles.'

'No, no! All right.'

'I'll get my purse.'

There were rules. Nance would buy them but they must be paid for.

Frances was up and dressed by the time they returned, sitting by the window; looking out but seeing nothing. A cigarette stub was still smouldering in the ashtray.

'Yo ho! We're back,' Nance called. 'I'll leave her in the pram for a while, she's nodded off. I expect it was all the excitement in the shop. Like pass the parcel it was! First Mrs Hodge behind the counter had to have a go and then everyone else wanted to hold her. She was *so* good.'

Frances smiled at her mother's pride.

'Phew! I'm worn out myself,' Nance announced, sinking back into the settee, still in her coat.

'Don't get over tired, Mum,' Frances fretted vaguely.

''Course not love. But I could do with a nice cuppa!'

Peta allowed Nance just sufficient time to finish the last drains of her cup before she stirred.

'Bless her . . . what timing!' her grandmother announced proudly. 'I thought I'd take her round to see the Masseys next door. They'd like to see her, and since I've taken her up to see Mrs Hodge I don't want them accusing me of favouritism.'

Frances smiled. 'Mother, you can do what you want so long as you don't want to show *me* off!' she said wryly. 'I'll get her ready for admiration.'

Nance, well used from years of practice at snatching sleep whenever and wherever she might, sank back into the chair and closed her eyes. She was dreamily aware of Frances' footsteps on the stairs and then the boards creaking intermittently overhead. Afterwards she recalled these details and that, when Frances had passed the baby to her, her eyes were misty, far away. At the time, though, Nance was just eager to get next door while Mr Massey was back home eating his lunch.

Nance had no real sense of anything wrong until she reached her front door. It was shut. Not so odd in itself and yet . . .? Peta was grumbling but something made Nance leave the baby in her pram in the garden while she went inside. 'Hello!' she called, but without confidence, not really expecting a reply.

The cottage was quiet, *very* quiet. Stale smoke hung in the air. 'Hello?' Nance called again, feeling panic rising. 'Anyone in?!' She stood uncertainly for a moment and then with a sudden surge of energy, rushed unthinking round the house, opening every door, every cupboard: nothing. *Nothing*. It was a relief and, for a moment she acknowledged this. Almost relaxing. *Not the worst it seemed*. But then . . . anxiety overtook her again. For the second time she panted up the stairs to the bedroom and this time noticed that Frances' coat was missing. She opened the wardrobe again . . . just a row of empty hangers clattering together with the movement!

Nance sat heavily on the bed. She could hear Peta outside crying angrily now. At that moment she saw the note propped up on the dressing table by the mirror.

'Give me a bit of time Mum. Please.'

Three times Nance read it before lifting her head. And as she did so, she saw the reflection of an old woman in a tweed overcoat, her face coloured with exertion, a wisp of loosened white hair trailing down her cheek. Sad somehow, and burdened, worried . . . and old. Yes, definitely that.

'Come on Nance!' She braced herself as Peta's wailings reached a crescendo. 'Not incapable yet my girl! It's relief you should be feeling . . . not the worst . . . and you've that precious little Petal all to yourself now.'

She never thought for a second that she should go after Frances.

Frances felt nothing complicated as she trudged along the country lane towards the main road, the hedges towering above her on either side like three-dimensional blinkers. No relief, but no regret either, only a feeling of forward energy, momentum, and the certainty that this had to be. No plans, no destination, just forward. That was all she knew.

To either side of her, in the dark hedges, tiny birds chattered and darted; shoots of white bryony and the

50

twined stalks of traveller's joy had broken through the dark earth, and the occasional dog rose quivered. Frances stood for a long time at the bus stop but still no one came to prevent her leaving, and she knew they would not. She was not impatient.

But when the bus finally arrived, snorting black fumes from its rear end, she realised that she hadn't even got her fare ready. Fortunately, someone was getting off, giving her the time to fumble in her purse.

She lifted her case up on to the bus, paid the fare and the doors whistled shut behind her.

May 1987

It was a sudden wakening into warmth, and sunlight, and cosiness . . . not a gradual hauling up from the depths. It was good to wake to the chatter of small birds nesting under the eaves, and with the noise of some heavy vehicle pulling away – the faintest and most distant sound. Strange that the curtains were open and the window flung wide. Ah yes, she remembered . . . in the night . . . the moon and the stars.

'Shut up birds!' Peta muttered, but grinning to herself.

Gradually she opened her eyes. It wasn't so bad after a while. She lay back on the pillow and stared up at the ceiling above her. There was a long cobweb trailing from one of the heavy beams. The lightshade, thick crinkled plastic fringed with silken tassels, swung gently in the breeze from the window. Peta moved the muscles of her face from side to side. The skin felt tight and crusty over her cheek and if she pulled her face as far sideways as she could she felt the skin stretching to breaking point. Gently she reached up and fingered the dried blood.

'Ah, yes. Umm.' She sighed, and threw back her bedclothes swinging her legs out of the warmth: Nance's winceyette nightie, the rucksack and the boots over by the chair, bloodstains on the pillow and a head like the inside of a drum.

'Yes,' she said out loud this time.

She sighed again and for one moment entertained the

thought of falling back into the dark but at that moment there came sounds of an intense squabble going on right outside the window. Two house martins were screaming at each other, their shadows flitting across the sunlit paths on the wooden floor.

'Hey! Cut it out you guys. Whatever it is, it's not worth fighting over,' Peta told them. 'What is it . . . a worm? A lover's tiff? The kids?' By the time she stuck her head out of the window it was all over. One bird flew one way, one the other. But they'd meet back here, under the eaves, sometime.

'That's the way to do it!' she said ruefully.

June 1973

Frances had returned, when she thought she was ready to, but not to Tom: to Peta, collecting her from Nance, who had watched them go with some misgivings.

'This is how it has to be,' Frances told Tom. It wasn't an explanation but there was something about her, her remoteness, the way she made him feel, that made it easier for him to protest but then move aside.

Then, with the money Nance gave her and after the settlement with Tom, Frances bought her 'box' as she called it, on the new estate, and resumed her part-time job at Kwick Kalls, the printers in the High Street. The robotic machines, the smell of the ink, the precision of the layout work kept her sane, she told Mollie, who looked after Peta while Frances worked.

It all flared up again quite unexpectedly, although deep down, somewhere, Tom had known it would. She wasn't right. *It* wasn't right for God's sake. This time he would have to say something. The baby that Frances held out to him that Saturday morning was almost unrecognisable. Gone were her precious baby curls, replaced by a severe pudding basin of a darker hue; she was dressed in navy-blue shorts with a strangely old-fashioned button-through shirt. He stared angrily at Frances, who was looking somewhere over his head.

'What's all this about?'

'Rain's stopped.'

'Frances, *answer me!* I've a right to know. She's my

daughter too you know. Why did you do it?!'

'Oh, it was getting in her eyes,' she answered vaguely, 'Don't you like it? It's much easier to keep.'

This was neither the time nor the place, and she knew it. He knew too, knew that he must swallow his anger until later. Peta herself pouted, silenced by the strange sounds and feelings stirring around her. She clung to Tom like a limpet. Nothing was different – as far as she was concerned at least – but every time Tom looked at her he felt his anger rise and Peta, sensing that her grin had somehow lost its magic, was crotchety all day.

It was with some relief but also some foreboding that Tom returned to the house later that afternoon and rang Frances' doorbell.

'Look . . . can I come in?'

Frances hesitated, then stood back from the door and motioned him inside. He followed her down the hallway along the rust coloured carpet to the living room at the far end. The room was decorated simply, he noted, in creams and browns, with a distinct absence of things at lower levels.

'I'll get her playpen. Take her for a moment.'

Peta, having just been reunited with her mother, and it being near the end of the day, started wriggling and crying when Tom took her back again. He wished she wouldn't. Frances would get quite the wrong impression. To distract her Tom pointed to their reflections in the framed mirror hanging over the fireplace.

'Look. Whossat?!' he enthused. 'Look Peta!' He grinned like a maniac, and the more he grinned the deeper Peta scowled; the more the little face in the mirror scowled back at her, the more miserable she became.

Seeing her bottom lip beginning to protrude and tremble again, Tom whisked her off to peer through the net curtains to the garden beyond, but not before his eye had been caught by the little silver-framed photo on the mantelpiece. It was an exact twin of the one in his own living room: Frances with their son in her arms, pudding-basin hair-cut, blue sailor-suit pants and a button-through shirt.

'Here we are!' Frances deposited Peta in her pen with a lego set, a selection of play people and a few cardboard books. Peta was not pleased and immediately stood up, shaking the bars and lifting one leg as though on the point of climbing out. And all the way through the ensuing argument Tom was aware of her presence.

'Well?' Frances lit a cigarette and sank back into a brown armchair. She put her head back and blew smoke rings into the air. As usual, she was coolly dressed, in well-cut cream cotton trousers, a toning shirt, sleeves rolled carefully back to show a gold chain bracelet. She crossed her legs, dangling one sandal from her painted toenails.

Although standing, and with his back to the mantel-piece, it was hard for Tom to feel as eloquent or as masterful as he had felt in rehearsal, whilst driving fast in his Cavalier.

'Look, Fanny . . . this has got to stop.'

She looked puzzled, 'What?'

'I mean, this is right out of line. Just what do you think you're doing to her, Fanny? OK so she's only a baby now, but what about her future? No . . . this has gone far enough. *No more!*' He sliced the air with his hand emphatically.

'What the hell are you on about Tom?'

Could her obtuseness be deliberate? It all seemed plain enough to him!

'Look, I've been reasonable. I let you take her. I agreed that she should stay with you . . .'

Frances snorted.

'Well, I *could* have caused a fuss,' he continued petulantly. 'Anyway, that's beside the point. The point is . . .'

'Oh do get to the point for heaven's sake!!'

His anger rose again. 'The point is . . .' he repeated, ignoring her, '. . . Peta is *my* daughter too . . .'

'Oh no, not that again.' Ash was about to fall from her cigarette and she cupped her hand carefully under it. 'Oh, pass me . . .' she nodded in the direction of the bookshelves. Exasperated, he held the heavy cut-glass ashtray out to her.

'Look Frances. I'm warning you, don't keep trying to put me off!'

'I'm not. I'm not!'

Was she almost laughing at him? He drew in a deep breath, shutting his ears to Peta's wailing, and his eyes to Frances' mocking stare. 'Peta is my daughter too. I have entrusted her to your care, Frances. You *are* responsible for her after all. But I think you're getting confused again somehow.' He hurried on – once started he couldn't stop – 'Maybe you're still ill and need help; but you can't go on pretending Frances. It's sick, just sick. Peter is long dead and gone!'

It missed him by the mere fraction of an inch. He could swear afterwards that he felt it graze his hair but perhaps it was just the rush of air. There followed, immediately, the deafening crash of shattering glass which fell in jagged pieces at his feet. One long second of utter shock, then Peta started screaming and so did Frances.

'Get out of my house! Leave me alone! I will do as I damn well please.'

And he went, at once, and without protest, stepping carefully over the slivers of glass.

April 1987

You can't tell me what to do! I will do as I damn well please!' Peta shouted at her mother.

'I will not have it Peta. *I will not have it!*' Frances told her in a low threatening voice, her hair peroxide now and with a false uniformity, still neatly in place despite the heat of the argument. Peta shook her own straggly hair and snorted at her mother contemptuously.

'And just how do you propose to stop me?' she sneered.

Why did it always have to be like this? OK, so she had been later back than she'd said. She'd forgotten hadn't she? Only remembered herself when she walked up to the front door. It was only the social at the hospital for God's sake. Not a sex orgy. Why did Frances have to make such a fuss? It had been just past nine when she'd walked in. Met a few friends on the way back. Got talking. That was all. So, the supper had been ruined. She wasn't hungry . . . Frances had been worried sick, but that was *her* problem. And no, Peta hadn't forgotten their phone number either.

It seemed a good moment to bring up the subject. After all, that was the issue wasn't it . . . being late, being out on the dangerous streets all alone.

'Look Peta,' Frances' tone was more measured now, more reasonable. 'It's you I'm thinking of . . .'

Peta laughed at her. 'Well, if that's so, let me remind you it's a bloody long walk from the hospital.'

'You know perfectly well what I think about you and

that hospital. Anyway, what's wrong with the bus?'

'Plenty.'

'I'm not arguing,' Frances told her, stubbing out a cigarette before continuing with quiet control. 'They're dangerous Peta. *Listen to me!* They're powerful and they're dangerous. More kids are killed by motorbikes than . . . anything,' she finished lamely. 'Mrs Frobisher's son lost both his legs in that accident last year. And she'll never forgive herself, poor woman.'

'Poor woman!' Peta repeated unkindly.

'Listen Peta, the answer is *NO*. And I don't want to hear another word about it.' She underlined the 'no' with both hands in the air and then marched firmly to the sideboard and poured herself a generous whisky, fingers shaking. She lit a cigarette with her large crystal lighter. Blowing cool blue smoke up to the ceiling, she sat lightly on the sofa and crossed her legs elegantly.

'And anyway, I can't bear to think of you roaring round like that. For God's sake Peta. Look at you! I can't stand the way your hair hangs into your eyes. I've told you, I'll treat you to a re-style and a new outfit of clothes for goodness sake.'

'I don't want new clothes . . . I like my hair like this! And I want a bike,' Peta replied quietly.

'NO!' Frances screamed, 'NO! NO! NO!' and she swirled round the room like a harpy, pointing her finger accusingly at her daughter.

Peta burst out laughing and dodged aside just as her mother flew at her. From outside the door she called back 'OK. I'll ask Dad then. I'm off to bed.'

Frances slumped back down onto the sofa, legs now inelegantly sprawled out, and sobbed into her arms until her mascara dissolved into two black smudges on her pale sleeves. But it hurt so much, all this crying. With a determined intake of breath she sat up again, took a tissue from the box on the table and blew her nose. She rose to check her make-up in the mirror over the

59

fireplace.

'Oh God!'

Using the same tissue she wiped under the rim of each eye, then paused. That little photo, she wondered why she kept it there, because it was so hard to look at, though sometimes she managed to clean the frame when it became too tarnished. And there was Peta's photograph. Not even framed, still in its brown cardboard surround, just as the school photographer had given it to her. Frances picked it up, smiled, and wiped the surface with her tissue. Snaggle-toothed, mischievous grin, hair unkempt, collar askew . . .

It had all been all right up till then, but now, now . . .

The next day Peta kicked at an empty beer can with a clean left sweep. It arched into the road and clattered down into the gutter twenty metres further down the street. She couldn't be bothered to go after it. Funny day it had been, just waiting for it to be over so she could go to Tom's. 'Course it wasn't anger any longer that morning, in the kitchen, when Frances stood briefly in the doorway to say she was off to work. Never *was* anger in the morning; it always changed to the wounded look. Anger's much easier to handle!

Tom would have finished work by now and be in the pub. Peta cupped her hand round the flame of her Zip lighter. The smoke she inhaled seemed to smother and extinguish the hateful feelings of pain and guilt. Chin up, jaw out, longer strides, hand thrust deep into the pocket of her camouflage trousers. *Goddamnit*, she wanted a bike! That was all. A bike. Simple!

She didn't go straight to the Rose and Crown but walked first to the fish and chip shop and bought thirty pence worth. She wasn't hungry, but the hot, fat chips seemed to settle something deep inside her. She stood in the street, leaning against the window and devoured them quickly while they were still hot.

From the distance came the roar of bike engines. Peta looked up quickly. Susuki GS 550, Honda 500 K. The two bikes tipped round the corner, veered towards her and screeched to a halt. Ken and Mike . . . had to be. She knew before they lifted their visors.

'Hey!'

'Hey!'

The boys straddled their machines without killing the engines.

'How ya doin'?!'

'OK.'

Mike twisted his handlebars, making his engine roar with fury.

'Where ya bin?' Peta asked.

'Around!' Ken shrugged.

She nodded, envious.

'Ah well. See ya!'

Ken backed his bike into the road, revved the engine and then released the brake so the bike reared into the air before speeding off, leaving Peta in a cloud of noise and burnt fumes. She screwed up her newspaper, wiped her fingers on it and chucked it, baseball style, into the bin outside the fish shop.

'Missed,' she said, with some satisfaction.

The Rose and Crown was already crowded. Phil Trap, the publican, polishing glasses behind the bar, sniffed loudly as if in warning as she approached.

'It's OK. I don't want a drink and I haven't got dog's muck on my shoes . . . more's the pity,' she added. 'I'm just looking for me dad.'

'Sorry. Can't help you.'

'Nobody can.' she laughed, and left.

Peta didn't like calling at Tom's house. Perhaps it was all too familiar, too comfortable, too much to do with her. Strangely Tom had never moved from the house he and Frances had first bought together. And finally Annette had just moved in with him. Tom was OK, she thought. He always had been; but tense, over-jovial, never seeming to know how to be or what to say. It was easier at home where she and Frances could scream and shout at each other.

Light on in the hall. Front curtains pulled across but carelessly leaving an edge of light. Someone's in! *Not Annette!* If she's in, I'm going.

Peta crept up the path like a burglar and put her eye to the window. In the gap between the fabric of the curtain and the wooden frame she could see the elongated image of Tom behind his paper. No sign of anyone else. Peta slipped round the back before ringing the bell. All was in darkness.

'Ah! Hello there. Well, well,' he greeted her brightly. 'Come on in!'

She strode in behind him, unbuttoning her jacket as she went.

'To what do I owe this?' he found himself asking before she'd even sat down.

Reaching inside her jacket for her cigarettes, she settled herself comfortably, folding one leg under her. 'Got an ashtray?'

She knew he hated her smoking. They used to row about it and now she never even asked if she might. He fetched a saucer and handed it to her without a word and then went over to open a top window.

'How's your mother?' he asked evenly.

'OK.'

'School? Going all right?'

'Yeah. S'pose so.'

That had covered nearly everything. She took a deep breath.

'Dad. Can you lend me some money?'

'Ah ha! Give or lend?'

'Give if you like!' she flashed him a winning smile.

'Well carry on. Convince me.'

She couldn't lie – strange that – not to either of them. Couldn't stomach it. However there were ways of manipulating, of getting her own way, which she *was* prepared to use.

'You see Dad . . .' she looked down, her fingers occupied in pulling a loose thread from her pullover and twining it round and round, '. . . I'm having a hard time with Mum, over deadlines and things, you know, getting in after parties . . .' she went on vaguely. He nodded encouragingly as she raised her eyes for a fleeting glance.

'Well, you see she's worried about me coming home late by myself. So am I really, but she wants me to be in *really* early so she doesn't worry, and I want to stay out late . . . well, not later than she wants me to . . . and, you see, we've been having all kinds of rows lately.'

He was beginning to look genuinely anxious.

'Anyway Dad, I want a motorbike and Mum won't give me the money.' Peta spat it out quickly.

'A motor bike!'

'Well, what's wrong with that?'

'Nothing . . . well, I suppose I'm not that keen on the idea either,' he admitted, springing up to freshen his drink. 'Do you want something?' he added as an afterthought.

'Umm . . . rum and coke.'

'Oh . . . coke! I think you've got me there, love.' He sorted through the assorted bottles on his trolley. 'No coke.'

'Oh anything . . . I don't care!'

'Vodka and lime it is then.'

He didn't mind her drinking, never had done, that was easy . . . but a motorbike!

'I know, I know. *So unladylike!!!*'

'No. I wasn't . . .' he began to protest.

'Yes you were. I know it. Look, I'm your daughter, you don't want me hanging around at all hours do you?'

'No of course not . . .'

'Well there we are then. I'm just offering you an easy way out . . . sleep deep, easy conscience!'

'Hardly.'

'*Please* Dad.'

She raised her head and gave him a very special eye to eye pleading. He melted.

'Well, what exactly did your mother say?'

She hesitated. 'Amongst other thing, she can't afford it.'

'Well, I don't know that I can.'

'Huh!'

'Oh, all right then, why not.'

Peta let out a cowboy whoop of joy and rushed over to Tom, throwing her arms around his neck. They were locked in a rare and bear-like embrace when Annette came in, still wearing her nurse's uniform.

'Oh sorry . . . don't let me interrupt,' she said as father and daughter sprang guiltily apart. 'What's the celebration?'

Peta lit a fresh cigarette. She was all right, was Annette, but she made Peta feel so big somehow, cumbersome.

'He's getting me a bike,' Peta boasted.

'Great idea. A bike! Good way to keep fit.'

'A motorbike,' Peta corrected her quickly.

'Oh.'

'I can see you don't approve,' interjected Tom guiltily.

'No, no . . . it's not really up to me to approve or disapprove is it?' Annette said, pulling off her coat and hat and shaking her hair free. 'Cuppa anyone? . . . oh, you're both drinking. Well, you'll have to excuse me . . . I'm dying for a cup myself.' She disappeared towards the kitchen leaving Peta and her father facing each other at either end of the carpet.

'Well, I'd better act fast before you change your mind,' Peta told him, buttoning herself into her jacket and draining her drink.

'Look. We'll have to go into all this, the "yes" was a "yes in theory",' Tom added, searching for a way out.

'Oh, any kind of yes will do me. I'll work out the details and send you the bill,' Peta said, stubbing her cigarette out in the saucer.

'Bye Dad, see you soon. Bye Annette,' she called from the hallway.

'Oh Peta, don't go because of me,' pleaded Annette from the kitchen.

'I'm not,' Peta yelled as she stepped out into the night.

Why can the looks on people's faces make you feel so bad? First Dad, then Annette. She tried not to see them but it was hard to pretend not to. Oh . . . rrr . . . she growled out loud and hunched her shoulders. Their feelings are *their* problems not mine, she tried to convince herself.

As she turned out of the front gate Peta swung away from home. There was no joy in the victory won somehow. No one she wanted to see. No where she wanted to go to . . . just the going, the walking, that was what she wanted most. That was the point of the bike. Not the safety-at-night-routine she'd appealed to her father's conscience with; nor was it the power and independence that she'd thrown at her mother.

Just to make going so much easier, going further too. And it wasn't where it was *from* or where it was *to*, just the bit in between. Soon – soon – there would be many junctions . . . lefts, rights, straight ons. All those decisions of the moment; thinking at speed.

But now . . . she looked up the road to the busy T-junction approaching. She already knew the decision would be left, on over the road and then up the lane to the hospital gates.

Jeff, the night porter, was an old friend. Peta

squashed her nose up against the glass and laughed as she saw him nearly tip off his chair with fright. He swiped at her with his rolled up *Express*.

He really shouldn't let her in, of course, rules and regulations. Nutty one she was, nutty as the inmates. They both agreed that. But, she was harmless. She liked to walk about the silent grounds under the dark cedars and yew trees between the red-brick hospital wings where the patients were sleeping. Anyway, he wasn't going to stop her. Big girl, with a temper on her. He settled back to his paper and turned the radio up.

Peta walked round the flower beds tended by the more reliable residents, over the grass to the dark shadow of an old cedar tree. Under its swooping branches the ground was soft and springy with loose packed needles. She pulled herself up on to the first branch and sat comfortably cradled in its massive hollow, her back resting on the ancient trunk. The bark beneath her had been worn light and smooth to touch in this crook of the tree and Peta liked to think of all the other bodies who, over the years, had sat here pulling strength from the solid wood, and perhaps leaving a little of their own. It was cold, bitter even, but Peta enjoyed enduring the pain of it and feeling it intensely, until suddenly it was nothing. There was no feeling left in her body, only in her head where life replayed itself. A slight wind teased the topmost branches though down near the ground all was deeply calm; her breathing filled with the perfume of earth and resin.

'Don't go because of me,' Annette had said, meaning she knew she'd interrupted father and daughter. Of course, it wasn't *that* at all . . . and yet in a way it *was* because of Annette.

She was all right, was Annette. Peta liked her even. But somehow, now, Peta didn't want to see her. She hadn't meant to say things to Annette, to let her in. She had felt better when they hadn't been so close. Wish I'd

66

just let it be, Peta thought, drumming her fingers on her leg. Feels better when they're outside your head; there's no room for them inside, not as well as yourself.

Settling herself more safely in the arms of the tree, she thought back to the last time she'd seen Annette – after that confrontation at school in September – and felt all the anger again.

That *stupid* new Year Head . . . her first day . . . what did she know . . . hauling Peta into her office and telling her she wasn't wearing the correct uniform!

'I want to see you in a skirt tomorrow Peta. Trousers are for the boys!' The way she'd said it, wagging her head from side to side, mouth all tight like a dog's bottom.

And then she'd gone and told Annette . . . thinking she'd be on nights Peta had climbed through the window in Tom's cloakroom and there Annette was, sitting in the kitchen having a cup of coffee . . . nearly jumped out of her skin . . . Peta smiled to remember. And then she'd told Annette how she'd gone berserk and thrown that stupid vase through the window, and how the heavies had come and thrown her off the premises.

That was OK. It was the questions that followed: why hadn't she gone home? What would Frances have thought? Why? Peta told her – *for about the millionth time* – that Frances would have to go up to the school, which she hated doing.

And Annette had said 'Why?' again, and that's when Peta had said more than she'd intended.

'Well . . .' she had begun, 'You know . . . facing it all. I don't mean seeing the Year Head, or paying the bill for the window. I mean . . . bigger things. Like facing who she is and her being my mum . . . slim attractive mother with big fat ugly daughter! And what the world says. And why it all happened like it did, and then wondering what to do about it – if it's not too late . . .

or if it matters anyway!'

And what was she going to do about it? Annette asked.

'Easy: mend the window, buy a new vase, say sorry . . . and then wear the trousers of course!!'

It wasn't much, but Annette always asked too many questions and Peta felt she had to answer them.

It wasn't like that with Tom. He was *easy*. Must have got it from him, she reflected. Never thinks about anything difficult. But I'm not really like him either, she thought; I bet he never sits in trees! Then again I'm not like Frances. How did they come to have me, she wondered? Like that time in chemistry when they'd put silver nitrate in a test-tube and added salt and they'd ended up with that thick white solid lump. She thought the experiment had gone wrong somehow. 'Thick white solid lump . . .' She repeated the words out loud into the night air. '. . . I wonder!'

Peta sighed deeply, and breathed a deep draught of cold pine-laden air. The branch below her was warm and strong and cradled her more comfortingly than any human limbs could. The chill in the air and her deep breath made her lungs suddenly convulse; she coughed and jerked forward and as she did so she became aware once more of the tree she was sitting in. She felt numb. Her bones she could feel, but not the flesh around them which felt more like insensitive sponge.

Experimentally she pinched her leg and felt nothing. 'Maybe I'm dead,' she said out loud, jumping down, her legs buckling beneath her, the blood rushing back to her feet like an excruciating electric shock. 'Ow!' she yelled. 'No . . . not dead!' Laughing, she limped away.

April 1987

Saturday! Peta groaned to herself. It would end in tears. It usually did, with Frances at home all day. All they seemed to do was bump into each other till the sparks flew. And since Tom's phonecall about the bike and the blistering scene that followed, the atmosphere had been strained to say the least. Neither the subject, nor the row had been referred to since. Maybe Frances was hoping the whole idea had died a death, but Peta knew it was only a matter of days now before her order would come through.

Perhaps, she thought to herself as she threw off the bedclothes, stretching and yawning loudly, it would be best if she spent the morning in the bath reading *Mad* and *Biker* magazines.

Peta was good with her feet and proud of it. When the water got cold, she pulled out the plug with her left foot and turned on the hot tap with her right, all without glancing up from the magazine propped on the plastic soap-rack which bridged the bath water. She could hear Frances hoovering downstairs and, when the hoovering stopped, the distant chatter of voices from the radio and the occasional slam of a door.

Twice Frances called up the stairs, 'Peta! Are you *still* in the bath?'

Peta didn't bother to answer. She picked up a bottle from the shelf nearby. The contents were bright blue. Peppermint. All right to suck on, but on your hair?! She liked to take lids off bottles of oils and bodycare preparations just to sniff, then hold them at arm's length in disgust.

Peta was a Vosene kind of person. At least it smelt clean, not like boiled sweets or blossoms. Frances said it reminded her of dogs, but as long as it was clean dogs Peta didn't mind.

She was kneeling in the bath, her hair a mass of white astringent lather when she heard Frances issue her final 'last warning'. Peta caught the irritation in her voice. She knew that disappearing into the bathroom for many hours was an irritating thing to do. Still, it was a good place to be while it lasted, a warm, wet refuge. Holding her nose she submerged her entire body for the ultimate rinse.

Frances, lugging the heavy vacuum cleaner up the stairs, paused at the top. The door to the bathroom was open and wisps of steam were escaping into the hall. Frances could see that Peta's arms were lifted over her head. She was towelling her back dry. She was quite naked. Frances stared, almost forcing herself to see, although she didn't want to. Then, when she broke away, quite suddenly, she found she was shaking, and could hardly fit the plug back into the socket.

Peta took *Biker* down to the kitchen with her. All hoovered and tidy now as though nobody lived there, and everything put away.

'Just have to get it all out again!' Peta said aloud, deliberately spreading out the bread, Flora, eggs, bacon, plates, knives and the honey pot in front of her. While the fat was heating in the frying pan, she took the top off the honey and dipped her finger in, lifting it quickly to let the honey dribble sweetly over her tongue.

'Ummm!'

Cardboard carton. Hateful. She levered one open, and tried to wash away the sweetness from the card-

70

board spout. As usual the milk dribbled down her shirt.

'Damn it!'

She was wiping away the traces with a J-cloth when Frances burst in. 'For God's sake, Peta. What are you doing now?' Red-faced from her exertions, her mother peeled off her marigold rubber gloves and flung open a window.

'It's my breakfast.'

'It's nearly one o'clock!'

'I still haven't had my breakfast!'

'Well, as I had mine at seven, I think *I'm* due for lunch!' Frances opened the fridge and brought out a tub of coleslaw and a fresh piece of blue-veined stilton.

'That fat's too hot.'

Peta turned her rashers over with a fork.

'A wooden spatula on that pan Peta . . . how many times . . .'

'I didn't touch the pan.' Peta slid the eggs on to a plate. 'Yum! Brilliant! Didn't break them. That's good luck!'

Mother and daughter sat opposite each other at the kitchen table. 'I can't enjoy my lunch with that awful smell!' Frances complained.

'I've warned you about that cheese before . . . if only you'd listen to me!' Peta countered.

Frances sighed. 'What are you doing today anyway? Any plans?'

'Why?' Peta was on her guard.

'Just wondering about supper, that's all.' Frances pushed her plate to one side and lit a cigarette.

'Oh, don't worry about me,' Peta said without irony, and then laughed. 'I mean . . . I'll be out I expect.'

'Oh, where?' Frances asked lightly.

'Party.'

'Oh.' She tapped ash into her saucer. 'What time does this party finish?'

'Oh God!' Peta got to her feet. 'Not this again.'

71

'I mean Peta, you are not to . . .' Frances stopped herself somehow, seeing Peta's mouth moving in mimicry. Changing her tone, she continued evenly: 'Midnight Peta. I mean it . . . and don't walk back alone, I won't have it. Midnight.' Before Peta could answer back, Frances stubbed out her cigarette, put the dish into the sink, lifted down her old padded jacket from her hook on the back of the door and silently left the house.

Peta could have stayed in and watched the racing or listened to that new Cure tape that David had pirated for her, but somehow she felt she'd rather be out. The High Street was thick with shoppers as she threaded her way between the laden baskets and the trailing children, dogs on leads, men going from the pub to the betting shop, groups of boys, united by their scarves and denims on their way to the match.

David would be working. Saturday afternoon peak time, stacking the shelves for the shoppers to empty, but at least she knew where to find him without having to see Mollie and the brats too. She saw him as soon as she rounded the corner of the aisle, sitting on the floor stamping the price on to each tin of Mr Dog with the natty gadget Peta coveted so much. Dog food in the new Super Store!!

'Give us a go!'

David's initial grin of recognition quickly faded. 'Get lost. Well . . . don't let him see you for God's sake . . . I nearly lost my job last time.'

Peta took the gun while he stood looking nervously to left and right.

'Just one.'

Peta laughed. 'You sound like my mother.'

She stamped half a dozen tins before handing it back. 'Rabbit flavoured! Yuk! Give me beef any day,' she drawled.

As David worked she sat on the freezer behind him.

'Faster! Faster!' She beat the sides of the cabinet with her heels, pretending to wield a whip over David as he worked. He smiled. The shoppers cast disapproving looks at her. David was laughing, but nervously and Peta knew that.

'Look . . . please . . .'

'OK, OK. I'm going. Just wondered, you going to Ken's party tonight?'

He shook his head vigorously, 'You know I hate parties!'

'Umm.' She trudged off up the aisle.

'I'm babysitting anyway,' he called after her. He was standing up now; his long grey coat almost reaching the floor. 'I'll get a video. Come round.'

Peta nodded as she turned the aisle head and walked back through cereals and biscuits to the check-out.

Peta didn't like parties either.

'But Saturday night is Saturday night!' she said to no one in particular as she put her cans on the table, detached one from its plastic circle and pulled the tag. Two girls in short skirts and high heels nudged each other and giggled. Peta took a long, thirsty gulp. There was Mike leaning against the cooker. He'd put his helmet on the shelf with the saucepans. She would have spoken to him but a girl from the year below her, trying to cover her youth with make-up, was standing next to him and everyone knew she fancied Mike. Peta moved through to the front room. It was jammed with people; some she knew, some she didn't. A few kids were dancing to Wham where Ken had rolled back the carpet. The light was shivering.

The back room was even worse. Lots of seats, settees, easy chairs, and every one occupied, with couples kissing and pawing at each other. There was Ken with his hand inside Alice Fairbrother's blouse, probably sitting in his father's favourite armchair too. As Peta turned, smiling to herself, she almost bumped into two giggling girls.

'Hiya!' she said affably.

It was enough to cause an explosion of laughter as they fell against each other clutching their sides.

It didn't usually worry Peta and probably she only imagined the last bit anyway, but part of her was sure she had heard one of the girls whisper '*Lessie!!*' Anyway . . . so what! . . . Stupid cows. What did they know, or matter?

When she squeezed her way back into the kitchen there was Mike sprawled all over the double burner with that fourth-year girl, her skirt so short you could see her knickers.

Peta didn't take just one can. She took the three, suprisingly still where she'd left them, and slipped out of the back door.

She had to put the two remaining cans away from sight before she went into the video club. Fortunately, her ex-army jacket was good for hiding things. Her eyes scanned the shelves. *Demons Three*. That would do. She knew David's taste well enough.

It was only a short walk from the video club in the High Street to David's house. She tucked the video tape inside her jacket and the lager cans swung from her hand as she walked. A dim light shone through the curtains. He'd be sitting there, already involved in his film. The upstairs lights were off, thank goodness! At least those two little horrors were dead to the world. She didn't ring the doorbell for fear of waking them but tapped three times on the window.

'I hate parties too,' was all she needed to say when David answered the door. 'Can't stand all those people.' It wasn't the people exactly, but, well, that would do.

David led the way into the living room. His video was on hold, Eddie Murphy's distorted face flickering as though palsied.

74

'I've brought *Demons Three!*' she told him, knowing David would stop his film and insert her choice instead. He would finish off his tape in the morning. He wasn't fussed, he was that sort of friend.

Peta knew he hated horror films too, the after-images haunting him for days while she would sleep deeply and untroubled. Still, he put it on without a murmur while Peta settled herself in Don's armchair and lit a cigarette.

Later, when Mollie and Don came in, the video was rewinding, the floor strewn with lager cans and crisp packets, and the ashtray was full. Fortunately Mollie was tipsy. Don, taking one look at Peta, locked himself in the downstairs lavatory.

'Oh my God, David.' Mollie stood in the doorway, steadying herself against the doorframe. 'What a mess!' As he scrambled around picking up debris and opening the window to let in the fresh night air, Peta diverted Mollie's attention.

'Look at you, all dressed up. Where've you been then?'

'Oh just a squash club social.'

'You look great!' Peta enthused.

'Oh, you think so?' Mollie, pleased, straightened up and pulled in her tummy muscles, her figure-hugging turquoise dress creased at the front. 'Glad to get out of these I can tell you,' she giggled as she kicked off her high heels. 'That's better. Get the blood back into my toes!'

'I don't know why you do it,' Peta said, looking at Mollie's pinched and misshapen feet.

'Vanity, dear, vanity. You'll understand one day!!'

'Hope not.'

'How's your mum?' Mollie asked suddenly.

'Ah . . . what's the time?' Peta replied.

Frances was still sitting in the living room in her dressing gown, and smoking.

75

'Oh God,' said Peta when she saw the anger in her face. 'No . . . I don't know what time it is. No . . . I haven't got my watch on. Yes . . . I did walk home alone. No . . . I didn't get mugged. Yes. I *am* sorry. Yes I am a pumpkin. Go to bed!'

But that wasn't enough to stop Frances. 'It's not good enough Peta. I was worried sick.'

So that was going to be the line tonight.

'I said sorry.'

'Sorry's not good enough!' Frances' tone rose. Peta shrugged.

'I won't have you roaming the streets at all hours. It's dangerous!'

'I'm OK.'

'This time maybe. But the streets are dangerous places for girls on their own . . . muggers, *and* rapists!'

Peta snorted.

'It's not funny!!'

'I'm not laughing. But I'm not likely to get hurt, am I?'

'Don't be silly.'

'I mean, who's going to take *me* on?'

'Shut up Peta.'

'That's one worry less for you . . .'

'*I said shut up!*'

'. . . and for both of us!' Peta paused and then continued lightly, 'And anyway, it won't happen again, I promise.'

Frances looked up suspiciously. Peta held her glare, 'Bike'll be here next week!'

Frances jumped to her feet. For a moment she looked as though she was going to slap Peta across the face, but instead she brushed quickly past her and raced up the stairs, leaving a cool draft of air circling Peta like a ghost.

May 1987

No doubt it was the bike which was responsible for the wall of silence that then fell between Peta and her mother. Still, she could put up with that. Certainly worth it for the ease with which she could speed away from it all. The roar of the engine and the scream of the tyres drowned the silence, and the energy, the vitality, the power of the machine swept away the stifling boredom of her existence. Peta paid heed to her mother's screams about the danger only in as far as to desist from smothering her crash helmet with stickers and slogans which might weaken its structure somehow.

Tom, guilty and chastened after receiving Frances' blistering attacks down the telephone, had bought Peta the most expensive helmet in the shop *and* a full suit of leathers. He then said he'd take the whole lot away from her if he found out that she'd had so much as a half of shandy before riding the bike.

'I trust you Peta . . . this is how I've chosen to show my trust,' he said, affecting himself almost to tears. In fact, he found his trust well-placed because Peta took her bike and her responsibilities most seriously. No kamikaze she; not waiting to be another adolescent statistic she rode with care for herself and her machine.

On Saturdays and Sundays she would meet with other bikers at the Maple Tree. Bikes would be lined up threateningly outside the cafe, marking territory in an unmistakable way, the owners enjoying the deferential respect given to them by the other patrons of the café who didn't own machines. Mostly though, they were given a wide berth, but an occasional child detached itself from its parents to move closer to admire.

There was much self-admiration too: of images reflected in the chrome and mirrors and helmets. And there was a cameraderie, of course, where each could be generous and open with their praise of other machines, gear, riding skills, and say things that otherwise couldn't be said. This mutual respect made them feel very close, very passionate.

Sunday lunchtime. Peta had just ridden into the tarmaced forecourt of the Maple Tree. She cut the engine, pulled the machine back on to its forks as though reigning in a horse, pulled off her gauntlets and eased her head out of her helmet. Mike was circling his bike over by the hedge but even at a distance she could see something was wrong. Quickly she pulled down the zippers on her boots, which flopped and jangled like a jester's costume as she strode over to investigate.

Little flecks had formed in the corners of his mouth like cuckoo spit.

'What's up?' she asked.

Mike spun round. 'Broke my mirror, man! *That's* what's up. *Broke my bloody mirror!!*' He carefully extracted a shard of glass from under the metal rim.

'Who did it then?' Peta asked.

'Dewey! The bastard!' he spat.

'Who's Dewey?' Peta asked.

'*Dewey*?! You know Dewey! From the Mardyke gang!'

'What was Dewey doing over this side of town?' At least she knew that Mardyke was the place where the kids on the north side of town hung out, cut off by the new bypass.

'Not here, dummy!' Mike shrieked at her. 'He wouldn't come over here would he? Outside my own

78

frigging house, that's where. Kid saw him. Just now it was, just half an hour ago!'

OK, OK. How am I supposed to know all this? she thought but didn't say.

'Come on then. What are we waiting for?' demanded Ken, buckling his helmet under his chin. 'Hop on.'

Mike obeyed, his anger suddenly diverted into activity, his eyes alight with revenge.

'Let's go!' he whooped.

'Hey! Wait for me!' Peta ran back to her bike, her loose boots clanking, pulling on her helmet as she did so, but Ken and Mike were already roaring off down the road and out of sight as Peta started her engine. She pulled the throttle out and the Yamaha, given its head, leapt beneath her, the speed plus the mission itself making her blood pump with excitement.

Even so, as she'd noted that the previous night's rain had left the roads greasy, she checked her speed as she cornered. Out on the strait of the nearly deserted Sunday highway, Mike and Ken had increased their lead. She hoped they wouldn't meet the cops.

She saw the leaf-green Rover approaching from the left-hand turning far ahead. Something, a premonition perhaps, made her tense and shout: 'Think bike!!'

She slammed on her brakes then skidded to an unnecessary halt a good two hundred metres away from the point of impact. She found she had clamped her gauntlets automatically over her helmet to try to cut out the sickening squeals of tyres and the sound of rending metals. She saw a puppet-like figure flung high into the air then she snapped her eyes shut against it.

'Oh no,' she found herself saying, and only after several seconds did she slowly prise her hands away and open her eyes to face the horrific quiet.

The first thing to break the silence was the green car door. A woman in a white sweater stepped out, a horrified look on her face.

'Oh my God, I'm so sorry' she said to Peta. 'I just didn't see them.'

'Stupid,' Peta yelled at her. 'You stupid, stupid woman!'

Ken was lying under the tangled bike, groaning and muttering, and recklessly Peta heaved the heavy bike off him.

He moaned, but his eyes flicked open and he recognised Peta. '*Mike*,' he mouthed.

Mike . . . Mike!! Where was Mike?! Peta looked around wildly.

'I just didn't see you . . .' the woman was still explaining to Ken, running her fingers round and round the gold chain at her neck.

There Mike was, lying crumpled in the gutter an unbelievably long way up the road. He was ominously still.

'Call an ambulance!' Peta screamed to the woman as she raced towards him. She slowed her pace as she reached him; there was something about the heaviness of his limbs, or perhaps the angle of his head, still in its big blue dome. Her mind suddenly filled with an image of a dead tabby cat she had found once in the gutter as a child. She had stroked it before her mother could stop her. Its body had been hard as ridged earth and ants were crawling out of its mouth.

Peta stood there, waiting for the ambulance to arrive. She turned away as the two men bent over him and cut through his blue helmet, one side of it smashed like papier mâché. They laid it gently on the kerb.

Two days later, after visiting Ken in the local hospital, Peta arrived home to find Frances standing rigid in the kitchen waiting for her. Peta couldn't tell whether she was going to hit her or kiss her.

'Why didn't you tell me?' she asked, her voice soft, not accusing.

Peta shrugged.

'Did you think I'd say I told you so?'

She shrugged again.

'My poor darling!' Frances came towards Peta, trying to hug her, but they no longer knew how to touch each other and both quickly broke away awkwardly.

'What can I say?' wailed Frances, wringing her hands.

'Nothing. Don't bother,' Peta replied, though gently.

Automatically Frances turned and filled the kettle from the tap, then plugged it into its socket. For a long moment Peta stared at her mother, seeing, almost feeling, the soft curve of her hips, her slim waist, the warm skin of her neck. It was like an ache. Then she looked away, and began picking at dried food on the tablecloth.

'Peta . . .' Frances began, then faltered.

'What?'

'Will it make any difference?' Peta lifted her head and stared quizzically at her mother. She knew what Frances meant but refused to understand.

'Of course it will!!'

'I mean . . .'

'I know what you mean,' Peta interrupted wearily. 'I always believed it anyway and now I know it, bikes *are* dangerous; that's all, OK?'

The kettle, boiling by now, switched itself off but Frances neither said anything further nor stirred herself to move, she just stood leaning against the sink.

'Goodnight!' Peta called from the bottom of the stairs.

Peta stood in her own room gazing out into the night sky, anaesthetised somehow. Her movements, when they finally came, were numbed and her limbs seemed far away. Slowly she pulled off her clothes, leaving them where they fell. Only last year she had redecorated her room, painting out the scenes from *Space Invaders* with three walls of matt-black paint. The fourth she had covered with sheets of aluminium foil, horrifying Frances, of course. The black had made a satisfying background for her posters of bikes and The Clash and she liked the foil wall for its strangely distorted shapes and images. There she was, like some kind of melted shape, blurred yet squatter, fatter, uglier. This image she could cope with, but there were no real mirrors in the room.

She turned on her radio. Some night music. Perversely she moved the dial until it picked up the crackled dialogue of a taxi fleet, then switched off the light and, naked, slid into bed, staring out into the urban orange night sky.

Under the sheet she folded her arms across her breasts and idly began to trace the contours of her own body. She gathered the handfuls of warmth from round her breasts and stomach and hips with no disgust. Then, with one hand, she gently curled wiry hair round her fingers.

'Roger? Rog . . . Come in Rog,' . . . crackle crackle . . .

'Roger here love . . .'

'Roger . . . got one for you,' crackle crackle.

'. . . that's what I like to hear,' . . . naughty giggles . . .

'Seriously Rog . . . go to the Marakesh, Oxford Road where a Mr Singh is waiting to go to the station . . .'

'OK. Willgo . . .' crackle crackle.

It was hard to get rid of the lifeless figure, the caved-in helmet and the sound of the impact which played over and over again in her head. And Ken, sobbing like a baby with his leg in traction, his head bandaged like a soldier from the First World War.

'It's my fault! It's my fault! I can't stand it,' Ken had choked.

'Lay off, man. Stupid word, fault. It just happened.'

'It didn't have to happen. If only I'd seen her . . . it didn't *have to* happen!!'

'It did. Somehow, it just did. You've got to get out of this thing,' she told him, surprising herself by saying it.

'It'll be months before I can walk again!' he wailed.

'I didn't mean that.'

'. . . and if ever I get my hands on that Dewey . . .' He clenched his fists, his eyes rolling oddly in their frame of white bandage.

'Forget it man.' It was all too backward-looking.

Ken looked at her as though at a traitor. 'I can't forget him man. It was his fault in the first place!'

Peta looked past him to the locker top. 'Is that what you drink out of or pee into?' indicating a bulb-shaped bottle tucked discreetly behind a vase of purple and yellow irises.

Ken was angry. 'Cut it out man!'

She shrugged; 'Gotta go', and picked up her helmet from the end of the bed.

There was something between pain and panic in Ken's eyes. 'Man! You're something else.'

She nodded and walked slowly down the ward aware of all the ill – and disapproving – eyes that followed her.

Fault . . . fault. She lay there in the dark, throwing the words into the dark room. Why did people have to say that stupid-sounding word anyway?! Fault! Isn't it bad enough? . . . He's gone . . . it happened . . . full stop . . . the end . . . And those if onlys . . . God! If only it hadn't rained; if only he'd seen the car; if only he hadn't made the suggestion in the first place! . . . If only the sky was pink, and rain was Coca Cola and earth was really chocolate and I was somebody else . . . and Frances loved me! Hah!

Peta beat the wall with her fist and let out a wild laugh. 'Yee . . . ha!!' she whooped like a cowboy, throwing an imaginary Stetson high into the air. 'An' don't you come back no more!' she told it.

She kept it hovering above her head just below the ceiling while her hand dropped down on to the bed. 'Go on then, up you go!!' and the hat flew through the plaster and the fretwork of wooden joists and lathes, through that gap which was neither floor nor ceiling, where the mice ran safely through the stuffy loft space spiked with invisible fibre glass, where the grey water-tank continuously filled and emptied. And then it flew higher; through the grey roof slates without disturbing them, and out into the cold air of night . . . up and up and up further into the inky-blue nothingness up towards the stars towards the moon . . . towards . . . yesterday and tomorrow and light and dark and fires and frosts. To the stars then more blue space . . . and beyond . . .

It usually worked. The objects she launched into orbit never reached anywhere, never returned, as far as she knew, because she was always asleep. Perhaps she did drift off, just for a minute or two but a scream of anguish woke her, chest thumping, eyes wide. Had it been Frances or had she herself made that weird cry? Or was it a cat in the garden? Automatically she turned the dial on her radio until she found the Night Owl and his music and bland inanities again. Had it been a cat? She went to the window and stared out into the orange night with its dark, dark garden. Nothing. Just nothingness.

Eventually she must have returned to bed and fallen asleep because she found herself snapping awake later with the pale dawn light in the room and the sound of an early blackbird outside. Propelled by a restless need to leave the house and just *move*, she pulled on yesterday's clothes and, carrying her noisy boots in her hand, she tiptoed downstairs. In the kitchen she opened the fridge, drinking a full pint of milk before quietly leaving through the back door. She left no note.

Having no watch, Peta wasn't surprised that she arrived late for school. She glanced at the speedometer. Over one hundred miles she'd covered. Kids appeared to be on the move, going from assemblies to tutor bases, to their lessons. She stood still, in a daze, by the bicycle sheds, trying desperately to orientate herself.

'Oi,' she called to a small boy in a large blazer who stopped and blinked nervously at her from behind round spectacles.

'What day is it?'

'Wednesday!' he replied and ran giggling back to his friends.

Wednesday, Wednesday . . . suddenly, she saw Ms Ashley flying down the steps, struggling under the weight of a huge ethnic basket bulging with books.

'Thank God!' she called as she caught sight of Peta. 'Carry these for me will you Peta? I'll take your helmet.' She said it in a way that made Peta wonder if she hadn't heard about Mike yet.

'Am I with you now?' Peta asked.

'Yes, dozy. It's Wednesday you know!'

When they reached the classroom Peta dumped the bag on the desk. 'I'm going for a wash.' she announced to Ms Ashley who was fortunately too flustered with handing out books, receiving late homework, sorting out worksheets and paper to respond.

The cold water felt good on Peta's eyes. She peeled off her jacket and trousers, slapping damp hands under her arms, and stood for a moment hugging herself, arms folded across her breasts. She smiled as she realised what an odd image she must seem, standing in a puddle of old clothes, dressed only in grey thermal underwear and biker's boots. Damn it . . . no change of shoes! No comb either! Ah well . . . she climbed back into the clothes, undid the zippers and then flopped back to the classroom which had by now settled down to reading quietly.

Ms Ashley looked up. 'Where have you been?'

'Washing . . .' The class tittered. '. . . You said I could!'

Ms Ashley had learnt more than to challenge Peta. She handed her a sheet and motioned her to her desk. 'Well, I suppose – for Peta's sake – I'd better start again!' A groan from the class.

'Don't bother.' Peta told her. But Ms Ashley did, of course.

Of all her teachers Peta had the easiest relationship with Ms Ashley. At least *she* didn't nag about trivial issues, and she didn't seem to dislike Peta either. She lost her temper sometimes, of course she did, usually when someone in the class started talking when they were supposed to be reading *Great Expectations* or some such. When she did get mad though, her voice rose and veins stuck out in her neck while bits of dark hair loosened themselves from the plait hanging down her back. Once Peta had burst out laughing at Ms Ashley in the middle of one of her tirades and to her surprise Ms Ashley had started laughing too. She had a lovely reading voice, soft, lulling, musical.

Peta put her head down on her arms and closed her eyes. At one stage she was vaguely aware of other people's voices. She even heard her name mentioned, and then someone said, 'I'd leave her if I was you Miss. Sleeping dogs . . .'

She'd gone far, far away, but now felt her arm being shaken so hard she couldn't ignore it.

'Peta, Peta! Wake up!' The classroom was empty apart from Ms Ashley who was standing over her anxiously.

'Are you all right Peta? You were right off there.'

'I'm fine. It's just your lessons, Miss!' Peta said,

yawning and stretching.

'Gee . . . thanks!!' Ms Ashley flicked at Peta's head with her fingers.

'What day is it?' Peta stood and stretched again.

'Wednesday . . . *still* Wednesday! The others have all gone off to Maths.'

Peta crumpled and sat down again.

'Go on Peta. It won't be that bad!'

'It will!' Peta answered, but stood again and clanked towards the door.

Ms Ashley held her head in her hands. 'Oh no Peta! Where are your shoes?'

Peta turned, shrugged, and made a grimace of help-lessness.

'Phone Michael's mum. Wake,' read the note propped against the teapot. Frances had long since given up waiting for her daughter, and had retired to her room with a good Ethel M. Dell. But she never rested properly, or even switched off her light, until she heard Peta's tread on the stairs and then the rush of the cistern.

It was too late for them somehow, for cosy chats. Frances had tried to get closer to her, make up for lost time somehow, but Peta was so unapproachable. How to begin? Anyway, now wasn't the right time, what with Michael's death and everything. Terrible to go through all that at such a young age.

Frances put her book aside, unread, sighing deeply. How she yearned to call out to Peta to comfort her, to talk about it all, mother and daughter. But even when she heard Peta move right past her door, she didn't dare. Peta would only stand in the doorway, fiddle awkward-ly with the doorknob, and avoid her gaze.

Even last night . . . those dreadful screams that tore her from sleep! Peta had been her first thought and she had wanted to rush to her, but knew it was impossible. She had stopped herself at the door, thinking that, after all, it had probably been a cat. She'd peered into the garden though, had seen nothing. Well, she wouldn't would she? . . . The cat was probably miles away and anyway it was far too dark!

'Why?' was not a question Frances often faced when something happened that just prized the lid off ever so slightly – the pressure always turned her rigid. With a sharp intake of breath she forced the lid down again. Yes, mistakes had been made, all right . . . of course. It had to be admitted . . . but that was all a long time ago now, wasn't it?

'It's not my fault. *It was never my fault!*' she would tell herself fiercely, struggling to force her thoughts on to a more manageable subject.

Had Peta found the note? Should she even have left it for her? Was it right to upset her, and at bedtime too? Perhaps she should have told Peta herself? It had distressed Frances, that call from Michael's mother. It had taken an age for the penny to drop – such a strong Irish brogue – and she hadn't realised who 'Mikey' was, or even what this 'party' was in aid of.

A party for goodness sake! And then when she'd realised, finally, Frances had turned all watery at the knees and blundered a few stupid words . . . how terribly sorry . . . such a tragedy . . . and yet she, of all people! Frances reached to her bedside table, found a packet of Benson and Hedges and lit one quickly. The smoke was soothing, though she really hated smoking in bed. There was an ashtray within reach, fortunately; near where she kept her earrings. Frances emptied them into her lap, played idly with them . . . pearl drops, tiny coral flowers like icing sugar, bolder gold fans and thick gold bands like signet rings.

A wake, she had called it. God spare the child, how grisly. But Peta doesn't *have* to go, for goodness sake . . . I'll tell her in the morning that she's to feel under no obligation. There is simply no need to go through all that . . . she can phone and explain . . . no, I know, Frances thought, I'll do it for her!

That resolution brought a smile to her lips, and she stubbed her cigarette out, put her earrings, the ashtray and her unopened book on to the table, switched off the light and settled down to sleep.

'But I want to go!'

Of course. Predictable really. As soon as Frances had made her offer, Peta had upset her again.

'Different anyway . . . day off school!' Peta had announced flippantly, causing Frances to slam down her cereal bowl in anger.

'We'll be having the wake on Thursday and then there'll be the funeral on the Friday morning. We've got Father Patrick himself to say mass for us. A lovely man he is and been so good to us all too, and such a favourite he was with Mikey when he was small. We do want you to come, Peta, as a friend to Mikey. I've heard him talk about you so often and I never got the chance to meet you till now, and his father and me, we do so want Mikey's friends to be there.'

When Peta had hung up the receiver in the old phone box she'd come across on her travels, she found herself really looking forward to the wake. She'd wanted to go anyway, not just to annoy Frances as Frances had obviously thought. Typical! Peta didn't know quite what to expect, but it seemed as though it might be fun in a way.

She parked her bike outside the house, squeezing it in between an old Rover which had seen better days and a gleaming new Sierra. As soon as she had removed her helmet she could hear the hum of voices and music: the 'party' already in full swing.

It wasn't difficult to identify Mike's mum either. As Peta stood, awkward for a moment on the doorstep, helmet under her arm, a small woman, her black hair fastened in old-fashioned rolls round her head, detached herself from a group of other women, all of them dressed in black.

'You must be Peta! Come in Peta dear . . . we'll be putting your helmet there on the hall stand next to Dad's trilby.' She smiled and linked her little arm through Peta's, leading her through the hallway which was packed, to a tiny 'cloakroom' as she euphemistically called it.

'You be taking off those hot things while I'll get you a drink. Is Guinness all right with you?' She was waiting outside the bathroom door with a tall glass hired from the pub filled with black liquid and topped with a thick creamy head: 'Now I'm wanting you should come and meet Mikey's Da, and Mikey's brother Sean who's come all the way down from Liverpool just.'

Peta gulped quickly at her drink and struggled through the mass of people squashed into the corridors and entrances of every room, through a pall of smoke and the wistful strains of Irish ballads. Mike's dad already had a shine to his nose and cheeks, and a slur on his tongue. He threw an affectionate arm round Peta, hugging her to him. Sean, towering over his dad, shook her hand in a powerful grip. Solid he stood, legs apart, obviously a firm base from which to throw the Guinness down his throat, one after another. Then, of course, there were all the aunts and all the uncles to meet; the whole London branch of the family come down by coach for the most part, and then the entire Irish lot, over on the night ferry from Rosslare.

It was when she squeezed her way out to the 'cloakroom' again, her insides feeling like an over-full water sack, that she bumped, quite literally, into Cousin Siobhan.

'It's occupied!' Siobhan told her. 'But there's another upstairs if you're desperate. I'll show you!' Family unmistakably, with those bright and bird-like looks and wiry toughness. Her eyes were jet beads. And she waited for Peta, sitting on the top step, clutching her knees to her chin.

When she came out Peta sat down beside her, looking down on the crush below. 'And you're Mikey's cousin of the fifth daughter of the third brother of Mikey's father's first wife!' Peta joked.

'He only had one! . . .' the girl replied quickly, but laughed too. 'No, I'm Siobhan, Mike's cousin.'

'And are you one of the boat people?'

'No!' Siobhan laughed again. 'I'm the London lot. And before you ask, I go to Hornsey Art College part of the time and work in a cake factory the rest of the time!' Peta was more interested in the cakes than the college.

'I put jam in the doughnuts. I've a big syringe of jam and I just give each of them an injection as they come past me along the line.'

'I love doughnuts! . . .' wailed Peta, '. . . I just love 'em!'

'And I can't abide them!' Siobhan confessed. 'Pity. I brought a big box down for me auntie but I think they're all gone now.'

'*Don't!*'

'Have you not eaten anything at all?'

Peta shook her head, suddenly ravenous.

'I'll see what I can find – hold on here.' Siobhan jumped up, straightening out her dungarees all crumpled from sitting.

Peta sat patiently. Her head light and her focus unsteady. Suddenly someone coughed behind her and she spun round.

'Psst!' An old man standing in the doorway to one of the bedrooms beckoned to her with a bony finger. 'Would you be wanting to see him young man?'

Out of curiosity, and certainly with no misunder-standing, Peta solemnly followed the old man into the room. He stood, respectfully at Mike's feet, dressed in what was obviously his best suit, with a tight-collared shirt and thin tie, hands clasped behind his back.

There he lay. In an open coffin. Newly varnished pine it was. He was barely recognisable in a cheap suit and shiny pointed shoes.

'We brought the gatelegged table up from downstairs. Devil of a job we had too,' the old man confided to Peta in a low whisper.

Two candles flickered at the head of the table on either side of the coffin and cast strange moving lights on Mike's face. It was hard to find here the boy she knew, dancing round in a fury with spit in the corners of his mouth. So young and childlike Mike looked now, his hair clean and curled over his forehead, his eyes closed, with long long lashes black against his pale cheeks. Strange, in spite of the smashed helmet, there was no mark on his head. Peta said nothing, felt nothing except curiosity.

'Oh yes, it was a tragic event, a tragic event. Such a lovely young boy he was. In the prime of his life too!' The quaver in the old man's voice made Peta feel uneasy and want to leave, but he caught her sleeve and would not let her pass.

'I'm Mikey's grandad, his mother's father. I lost my dear wife of twenty-nine years just this last year past, of the fever . . . and now my youngest grandson too.'

Allowing herself just a brief glance into the old man's face, Peta saw tears rolling down his sunken cheeks and, guiltily, she eased his grip on her arm. Then without another look at the coffin, she slipped out of the door.

Siobhan stood at the top of the stairs holding two flaking and rather limp sausage rolls in her hand.

'Oh Lord! Did he come and get you? . . .' she asked sympathetically. '. . . I wouldn't go in myself!'

Side by side they sat, filling and refilling their glasses

but otherwise not talking much or laughing, just being silent and comfortable with each other. It was much later that Mike's mother found them, heads on each other's shoulders, slumped against the newel post at the top of the stairs.

'Wake up. Wake up!' she said, shaking Peta's arm. 'Time to be off home now, Peta . . . I'll get one of the men to walk you back, because riding that bike I forbid. Trouble is . . .' she wiped her forehead unsteadily, '. . . they're all a bit . . . well, it's a hard time for us all now.'

'I'll walk home with her, Auntie,' Siobhan offered. 'It's fine. I'm a big tough London girl now, don't you fret.'

Mike's mother's thoughts had already left them as she moved away saying quietly, 'Well, I'll just be looking in on Mikey now . . . to say goodnight.'

Later, Peta remembered only fragments of the walk home through the quiet streets, lurching from pool of light to pool of light, leaning against lampposts, arms round each other. Then there was a lingering sensation of falling back on to her bed and laughing as Siobhan struggled to pull her boots off. But that was all, and so it was a shock to wake, opening her eyes to a strange head of short-cropped hair on the pillow beside her.

Slowly she reconnected with distant parts of her body and as she did so she became aware, inch by inch, of another human body neatly curled into her own. A current of panic sent her rigid. Siobhan stirred, mumbled something and flung a sleepy arm over Peta's body.

As the thumping of her head gradually dominated the beating of her heart, Peta closed her eyes again. 'Oh, what the hell!' she sighed, and rolled over and back into sleep.

Tap, tap, tap, tap on the door.

'Peta. Peta. Wake up. It's nearly ten!' Frances, her ear to the keyhole, could hear nothing. She had heard the key in the lock the night before and the uneven, heavy tread on the stairs before relaxing into sleep herself. At least, she thought she had, but had she dreamt it? Perhaps Peta had not come home at all? Surely she should open the door just a crack to reassure herself, breaking *all* the house rules. So Frances did and found herself face to face with her own nightmare. Her screams woke Siobhan and Peta more effectively than cold water could have. They both sat bolt upright, staring at Frances who was dancing hysterically in the doorway.

'Oh my God . . . oh my God! Get her out of here! How could you? . . . *in my house!* Under my roof! *Get her out of here!* . . . You . . . you . . . you!!!'

The hysteria of her words hung all around until quietly Peta, fully clad, got out of bed and pushed Frances firmly out of the door, closed it, and leant against it . . .

Mike's funeral too; head like a drum, tongue like old velvet curtains . . .

Siobhan stood by the window smoothing the creases out of her dungarees with one hand and sleepy dust from the corners of her eyes with the other.

'Can I have a wash?' she asked, and they smiled at each other.

Tentatively Peta open the door again, half expecting to see her mother crumpled theatrically on the landing, but she'd gone. In fact Frances had left the house, so they were able to drink a pot of tea and settle their gnawing stomachs with wedges of bread and peanut butter. Nothing was said between them, partly because it was too much effort to speak and partly because neither knew exactly what to say.

At the fork in the road Siobhan said, 'I'd better go straight there.'

'I'll get my bike first,' Peta told her.

Mike's house was quiet, forlorn looking with all the

curtains drawn in the windows and the broken gate hanging on one hinge. A few bright yellow dandelions waved cheerfully on long stems in the neglected front garden.

As Peta hooked her bike off its forks a neighbour in a pinny ran down her garden path waving at her. 'Have you come for Michael?' she called.

Peta was confused. 'He's dead!'

'Oh well, yes. That's what I was going to mention,' the woman said. 'They're burying him right now.'

Peta – though she realised she was late – drove very carefully. It seemed wrong to take this noise, the bike too, into the quiet of the graveside. Better leave it on a side road and walk. But just as she was parking it on the corner by a neatly trimmed privet hedge, an old man came to the garden gate and shouted at her.

'Oi! You! You can't go leaving that thing here! This is a respectable neighbourhood!' His face was an unhealthy red and his arms, protruding from rolled shirt-sleeves were pale and stringy. Two elderly women appeared on the front porch behind him, one in an apron, the other wearing gardening gloves and waving a pair of secateurs.

'It's all right, Albert. He's doing no harm!' they reassured him.

Without comment Peta turned towards the cemetery gates. She'd been before, of course, with her mother, to the farthest corner beyond the dark yew trees, though not for some time now. But it was on the other side of the cemetery that the figures had gathered now, heads bowed. They stood with their backs to her and she could not see the earth or where they were staring. She hung back, leaning against a sturdy weeping angel.

Mike's grandpa supported by two of his daughters, one of them probably Siobhan's mum. Mike's father with his six brothers and sisters, their wives, husbands, children. The headmaster. Ms Ashley, arm round the fourth-year girl Peta had seen with Mike at Ken's party. Some other kids too . . . the bikers . . . but not Ken of course. Father Patrick in his long gown, obviously saying something but his words were carried away in the wind and Peta could hear nothing. Ah, there was Siobhan leaning forward, her arm tucked into her mother's and resting her cheek on her mother's sleeve.

. . . *Siobhan's cheek on her jacket, or was it* her *cheek on Siobhan's jacket? or was it Frances' jacket, the one with the velvet buttons which Peta loved the feel of so much? . . . but whenever she had smoothed her skin against her, Frances had wriggled free: 'Get off me Peta! You're wearing me thin!'*

The adrenalin seemed to shoot up through Peta from the very ground she was standing on, and by the time she reached her bike she was running hard.

Leave the bike in the garage, safe enough there. They'd better be out: can't face them! Car's gone . . . *please* don't be here!! Window's open . . . can get in then. No one in the kitchen this time. *Feels* empty. Keep moving . . . keep moving! Need the rucksack . . . should be under the stairs. Don't stop now; *don't stop*. Take an old jumper or something. Up to the bedroom. Great. This'll do, he won't miss it. Better leave a note. Always a pad by the telephone . . . pencil . . . pencil . . . in the drawer? *Great!* . . . cash stash! Borrow a few notes: 'Look after the bike for a bit. Thanks for the money.'

Put the note in the helmet and the helmet on her bed; they're bound to see it. Leave the drawer open too: doesn't look so sneaky. Right, all set. Anything else? Just grab a bottle downstairs. Bells, that'll do. That'll help. Don't want to think; *don't want to think*. Now . . . just one quick pee . . .

At first she thought it was just the blood thumping through her body but, no, the sounds were definitely getting louder. Footsteps. The creak of a gate, a low cough and then the distant fumbling of a key in the lock.

It was Tom! In a wild panic Peta leapt up, pulling at her trousers and, without hesitating, flung the window wide. Maybe it was her haste, or perhaps the trembling, that made her foot slip on the basin and sent her crashing forward into the frosted glass. She felt the pain on her face as though she had been hit, lost her breath for a second as her ribcage smashed hard against the window-sill on her way out. But it was only a matter of seconds that she lay there, stunned, before she picked herself up from the earth and was running down the street, holding one of Tom's old shirts to her face to staunch the blood.

May 1987

The warm spring sun was flooding the room, dust was dancing in the threads of light like fairies. Nance, unaccustomed to sleeping in this late, took a full minute or two to organise her thoughts . . . 'An extra pint or two of milk, if I can catch Mr Jenkins!' Oliver stretched luxuriously, approving of the new, less rigorous regime.

The empty bottle was still lying on its side on the front step, presumably where Peta had kicked it over the night before. Nance righted it and stuffed Mr Jenkins' note inside the neck. It was a glorious day. A fall of rain in the night had left the world clean, newly-washed; drops of water, caught on the plants and grasses, reflected the sun like a million tiny mirrors.

I'll have to get some kindling from the shed, thought Nance, poking at a potential bonfire – a pile of dead wood and briars cut recently from behind her vegetable patch. Her little plants were all coming on well too; the beets, purple-veined as if with blood, the feathered carrots, the broad beans fairly springing up. No sign of peas yet . . . a little worrying; perhaps a dud packet. 'One more week I'll give you!' she threatened.

A tap-tapping at the window made her turn. Peta! Peeping through the faded gingham curtains at the upstairs window, waving . . . so childlike, it was hard to believe. She was still puffy with sleep when she joined Nance at the back door. She blinked at the light and yawned and stretched as indulgently as Oliver, then grandmother and granddaughter stood, arms round each other's waists while Nance pointed out this year's gardening triumphs and disappointments.

Peta was shivering. 'Come on now, you're cold,' Nance said. 'Look at the pair of us, still in our night-gowns at ten in the morning. This could constitute a scandal in the village if ever it was to get out!!'

Peta laughed: 'I love this village. I wish I lived here . . . nothing ever happens, it's always the same.'

'Listen to your voice . . .' Nance exclaimed, horri-fied.

'It's always like this in the mornings. Down in my boots . . .' Peta told her cheerfully. '. . . You ain't heard nothing yet!' she promised, and coughed a thick, tobacco cough.

'Good heavens. What a sound! At your age too. You need the good country air in those lungs . . .'

Peta nodded.

'And your face, my Petal. Is it sore?'

Peta shook her head. 'Messed up the pillow-case though, I'm afraid.'

Nance liked to fuss and Peta allowed it. Back inside Nance sat on a high-back chair while Peta sat on the floor in front of her. A grooming session, hair brushed until it shone, and Peta quietly eating her toast. 'There now – look at the gloss on that – if only I had a slide or something . . .'

Peta shook herself free with a yelp. 'No hair slides! There I do draw the line!!'

'You always did.' Nance busied herself pulling the dead hair free from the bristles.

'What about my clothes?' Peta wailed, suddenly remembering. 'I've nothing to wear.'

Nance put her finger to her nose. 'I have the very thing,' she promised.

Together they climbed the steep stairs to the attic room. Over by the window was the wooden chest where Peta had been kneeling the night before. Nance opened it and pulled out from the very bottom, still folded in leaves of tissue, two of her husband's dress-shirts. Good quality cotton they were too, with their starched fronts and long backs. 'Good tucker-inners', he had called them. Nance had not been able to give these away when she got rid of his everyday clothes, but had stowed them away quietly like a secret. She sighed just once as she unwrapped them. She shook one out and handed it to Peta, but the other she quickly hid back in the chest. Delighted, Peta slipped the shirt over her head. The tail fell like a dress to her knees and the neck and cuffs flapped open without their studs.

'We'll just have to wash your trousers. They'll dry in no time in this sun. Socks they sell in Mrs Hodge's shop and the rest we'll just beg, borrow or steal. *And* we can still have our bonfire!!'

Word had travelled round the village, probably carried on the milk float, that Peta was back, and no eyebrows were raised later when Nance put two pairs of nylon-mix men's socks into her shopping bag, or when she asked Mrs Hodge what size feet her husband had.

Bonfire smoke was seen rising, a clear signal, from behind the cottage. It blew over the fields behind the Masseys' farmhouse, and evening brought Mrs Massey out with an old pair of her father-in-law's brogues and some grey flannels.

'They are only sevens. Small feet on that side of the family,' she told Peta, handing over the shoes. She and Nance were sitting having a 'lap-supper' in front of the TV, Peta still wearing only the dress-shirt.

'And I've disturbed your meal too!' Mrs Massey added apologetically.

'No, no, just a cold salad,' Nance told her, switching off the set.

Peta already had the brogues on her feet, a good fit they all agreed.

'And I've these flannels too,' Mrs Massey hesitated, eyeing Peta's bare legs. 'They might tide you over so to speak. They're a bit massive, so I've put the braces in as well.'

Peta held out the huge trousers in amazement. 'But won't he be wanting them?' she asked.

Mrs Massey laughed out loud. 'Dear Lord, he will not!'

'He died last year,' Nance added quietly.

'Oh. I can't imagine old Mr Massey being gone . . .' Peta said. '. . . He's always been there.'

'Well, that's certainly what it felt like, I can tell you!' Mrs Massey was enjoying herself. 'Still,' she continued in a more sober tone, 'he had a good innings.'

Dressed in 'dead men's clothes' as Peta referred to them, she and her grandmother were now able to venture out of the house together. They went together to Mrs Hodge's shop, causing a minor stir; and later Peta bought Nance a sweet sherry at the George, both of them weathering the scandalised looks and the nosy intrusions.

As in the old days, Peta fetched the cows in for Mr Massey and helped wash their teats before he fixed the electric milkers on to them. But mostly Peta sat in the little button-back armchair with Oliver on her lap, and read her way through Nance's old D.E. Stevensons and Dorothy Sayers, just biding her time. She noticed of course, when Nance got agitated, sorted out ten pence pieces from her purse, and then set off for the village shop, returning, apparently, with nothing. Peta knew time was passing by the way the ugly gash on her face was healing, and as she healed on the outside the same healing process seemed to be happening somewhere deep inside her too.

'Quite pretty!' she pronounced the new and delicate pink skin magically there when she picked off the scab. Though she didn't as a rule like mirrors she found herself more and more interested in talking to the person she found looking back at her from the little tilted mirror which stood on the dressing table.

'You may not look it, but I know you're tough,' she told the scar, or maybe herself.

It took the time it took. Then, one day she looked at herself, eyeball to eyeball, and said 'You're OK. Anyway, I'm stuck with you, but I think we're going to be all right somehow!'

Nance and her secret phonecalls were working out the details Peta knew, and that was all right for a while. It was not yet the time for questions, and Nance told her nothing.

June 1987

Peta was on the point of ringing the doorbell when she heard the unmistakable sound of voices raised in argument coming from inside. She paused a moment to listen.

'Ten years, Tom! *Ten years!* That's how long we've been together and ten years is a bloody long time to wait!!' she heard Annette say in an unusually passionate tone. 'I understand . . .' her voice had dropped and Peta missed the next few words; '. . . but it's not going to dominate my life too!!'

Peta hit the bell. It wasn't a habit of hers to stand and overhear snatches of conversations which might burden her: the less she knew, the safer she felt.

Tom came slowly to the door. 'Good timing!' he said, perhaps ironically; 'As usual!'

'*Tom!*' Annette called reproachfully from the kitchen.

'Sorry love,' Tom apologised to Peta; 'Good to see you. Here, let me take the sack . . . hey, that looks familiar!' Peta grinned at him.

'Hi Peta!' Annette called. 'Come on in. We've kept your lunch. Nance said about noon actually, so . . .'

'Oh, I missed the early bus,' Peta explained vaguely.

'Not to worry. Just pop it in the micro!' he said jovially.

'The what?'

'I know!' Annette apologised, peeling clingfilm from the dispenser on the wall in front of her, 'A present to the busy working housewife from the independent professional working woman. It's great. Now Tom has no excuse at all; *he* can heat a frozen dinner as well as I can!' and she laughed.

Peta smiled with her, and with relief. A rift between Tom and Annette had not featured in her calculations. Annette made her feel at ease too; and she wasn't going to probe it seemed. She was back there, in her life where she belonged, and it felt fine.

Calculations, plans, The Future . . . it had had to happen. Finally Peta knew that she was ready. She new Nance was waiting for her, though she wouldn't hurry her.

'OK. Nance, what's going to happen to me eh?' Oliver stretched across her lap, purring loudly, his eyes closed, the tip of his tail flicking from side to side as Peta rubbed the fur on his stomach. It was dangerous, they both knew this; the back was safe, but the stomach . . . at any moment he might turn savage, curl round her hand like a glove and bite and kick with his back legs. Peta enjoyed the suspense.

'Well dear.' The moment Nance had been so waiting for now clearly took her aback. She sat rather precariously on the arm of the sofa. She was in the middle of preparing their supper and her pinafore was covered in flour, as were her hands.

'Well, I don't know what you're going to think about all this,' she hesitated, 'Perhaps you'll just think I'm a meddlesome old fool.'

'Of course!!' Peta grinned up at her from her tussle on the floor with Oliver.

'I don't want you to think we've all been going behind your back . . .' Nance persisted.

'Well, you have! But I've got eyes in the back of my head too, don't forget. So just tell me what I'm going to do, and I'll get on and do it.'

Nance took a deep breath. 'School. They'll let you go

back and take those exams.'

'Big of them.'

'You never know what the future might hold, Pet. We want to open all the doors we can, don't we?'

'Oh I'm in favour of open doors!'

No argument. Nance blew the air out of her cheeks in relief.

Peta settled back in her chair. 'So tell me more about these doors!'

Nance spread her arms, palms to the ceiling. 'Who knows, Petal. Who knows. But if you tuck those exams under your belt that'll take us to the next stage . . .' she hurried on, '. . . and everything will fall into place, believe you me Pet. I know it will.'

'OK. To the next stage!' Peta announced theatrically, pointing her finger straight at the front door. Nance smiled. Oliver twitched his ears.

'And in the meantime? . . . Let's hear it . . . .' Peta was prepared to fight on the next point. She could not go back to Frances . . . on that she was adamant. But no fight was necessary; Tom and Annette would have her – on a *temporary* basis, Tom had asked Nance to stress that.

'Poor Dad, always been terrified of me!' Peta laughed.

'Well just you be kind to him. None of this is his fault . . . not really.' There was a tinge of doubt in Nance's voice which Peta recognised.

'Stupid word, fault!'

'Well I agree Pet, I agree,' Nance said soothingly.

'Hope you're hungry!' Annette said now as she slid a plate of cold and congealed macaroni cheese into the new oven. It whirred like a time bomb and in a ridiculously short time the bell rang and the macaroni was transformed, bubbling and appetising. Annette reached in and took hold of the plate with no gloves.

'Don't trust it myself,' boasted Tom. 'I always use

oven gloves myself.'

Peta sat at the kitchen table and ate hungrily. Annette pulled out one of the pine stools and motioned Tom on to another. 'So,' she began searching for conversation. 'How was the journey?'

'Fine. Except I missed the bus!'

'Ah yes . . .'

Pause.

'. . . And Nance?'

'Fine. Did you know old Mr Massey died?' Peta asked suddenly.

Tom frowned. 'Now, remind me, who were the Masseys?'

'These are his shoes!' She stuck out the brown brogues.

'Stout,' Annette conceded.

'Hey, good golfing shoes!'

'No way!!' Peta tucked them back under the chair.

'A temporary measure. A temporary measure!!' she repeated to herself that evening as she brushed her teeth. They'd had the bathroom redecorated in white and green – white paper with small minty leaves, the skirting board glossy and green – Annette, no doubt. A bidet too. Try it out; and why not? Fill it with hand-warm water . . . better go easy here! Pull down the trousers . . . where's the soap? . . . green, of course, pine. Kind of antiseptic smell . . . what the hell does pine smell like anyway? here goes . . . the rim's a bit cold . . . nice though that . . . that warm water . . . good feeling and with that smooth green soap . . . *Do your own cracks!'* . . . that's what Nance used to say . . . '*Dried your cracks? If you don't get the talc in those cracks they'll get sore,'* . . . funny what sticks in your mind . . .

Damn, haven't got a towel. Oh well, this one will do, green, of course, and fleecy-warm too from the radiator. What a mass of great sensations. A hot towel in your cracks! Just need that talc . . . could be in the cabinet over the wash basin. Shaving soap, eye-drops, tincture of iodine, antiseptic cream, hair-removing cream . . . no talc. What's that on the top? Wallets of pills, all stamped: 'Tagget's the Chemists', dated January, February, March. And all full too. The foil backing was still intact, the little yellow pills rattling slightly in their clear and sterile bubbles. Peta refolded the wallets carefully, replacing them on the top shelf.

'Tinkering', Tom called it. A whole day it took her to get the bike working again. On the second day she rode it in to school. Not to attend classes, that could wait. No, for something more important. The careers teacher was sitting in his office when she entered the room and started leafing through the handouts neatly fanned out on the low coffee tables, and studying the enthusiastic posters on the walls.

Mr Jackson watched her suspiciously. He checked the diary on the desk in front of him.

'You haven't got an appointment, Piper.'

'Got a pen?' she called over to him.

'A pen?'

'Yes, you know . . . thing to write with.'

'Don't be clever with me!'

'Well, have you?'

'Of course I have!'

'Well. Could I possibly borrow it then? Hmmmm?' she asked with mock servility.

Annoyed, he reached into his blazer pocket and automatically clicked the ballpoint into position for her.

'Hey, fancy!' She wrote the number quickly on the back of her hand, retracted the point with an over-dramatic gesture, and returned it to him with a bow.

Without further comment he replaced the pen, but she noticed that he'd reached for the phone by the time she got to the door.

'Pathetic!' she called back to him.

Fortunately, the voice on the other end of the telephone was more helpful. Yes, openings for males *and* females – good career prospects for go-ahead youngsters with initiative and common sense. Yes, there was a small test – English *and* sums – not so interested in that side of things! Still, it does help if you can read notices. *Danger this field is mined!* Things like that! *And count the bullets left in your magazine!* So, come on down . . . meet the OIC – Officer in Charge – he'll fill you in, *and* fix you up!

The phone booth Peta had chosen was directly outside the hospital gates. She was really on her way to see Janie and Mavis and Lil, but she knew they would make her wash her hands and then she'd lose the number.

It had been ages since she'd even thought of Janie. Bad feeling that. She'd really let her down. Bad! Mavis and Lil would understand, that was all right, but Janie wouldn't. Couldn't. Peta thrust her hands deep into her pockets and walked, shoulders hunched, head down, thinking.

'Lord love us!' Lil had said after they'd met up noisily and joyously in the office. 'Don't you be thinking like that at all . . . She's not *able* to understand chicken!'

'Exactly! So . . .' Peta took another drag on her cigarette, '. . . she hasn't missed me then?'

'I didn't say that!' Lil said quickly. Mavis was shaking her head sadly.

'That's her now, screamin' and a screamin' and carryin' on. Come on Peta, let's go in and see her now before Jimmy comes to takes them all off for lunch.'

There Janie sat in the far corner of the room. Someone had tied her hair back with an old-fashioned white bow. Kneeling at her side was a young auxiliary nurse in a green overall who was attempting to interest her in a pile of coloured bricks, but Janie's eyes were rolling this way and that . . . any way but in the direction of the bricks. Her tongue lolled forward out of her mouth, her back rigid and her legs straight out at right angles with her torso. The nurse was pressing a brick into her hand.

'Come on, Janie love, put it on the tower.'

Simultaneously Janie threw her head back and the brick forward with all her force, and let a bloodcurdling scream rip from her throat.

'Oh God,' sighed the nurse; 'Sorry,' she apologised to everyone else in the room.

'*Oh Janie!*' scolded Mavis, darting forward to help. 'And I don't know why you should be saying sorry,' she told the nurse who was quietly packing the fallen bricks away in their box. Peta slipped back into the deserted office. She filled the kettle, rinsed the cups and automatically sniffed at the milk; not quite fresh but not really cheesy either. Maybe if I hadn't vanished like that, she thought. Maybe? Oh maybe *what*? Maybe Janie would be able to put a yellow building block on top of a red one. So what. *So what*?

'What's it all about anyway?' she asked her image upside down in the teaspoon.

'I never ask myself my love. So long as I get my money at the end of the week and Reg and I get our steak and roly-poly on a Saturday night I'm happy,' Lil winked, coming into the office.

'Glad someone is!' said Mavis wearily, following Lil into the room in time to catch the tail end of her confession. 'I'm worn to a frazzle, I am. Don't ask me why. Oh there's my girl,' she said as she took the mug of tea from Peta. 'We've missed you.'

'Glad someone has!'

'Fishing, always fishing, that Peta. Give us another sugar love, no, make it a couple,' said Lil.

'How's the diet then?'

'Oh *that*. What the hell. Fat and happy, that's what I always say!'

'I'll drink to that,' Peta raised her mug.

'Well, spill the beans. What's been happening then?' Lil was dying to know.

'Oh nothing very much,' answered Peta evasively.

'Don't give me that. Was it Prince Charming then? Swept you off your feet like I told you?!' Lil went on, kicking off her shoes and wiggling her toes round in her stockinged feet.

Peta laughed aloud. 'Not exactly! No, went to me nan's and now I'm at my dad's — that's the short version!'

'Oh, your poor ma,' sighed Mavis predictably. 'She must be a sad woman.'

Peta lit herself another cigarette as she considered this. 'Yep, you're probably right Mave. But I'm going to look after number one now.' She put on her cowboy drawl. It was hard to say it straight.

'Well, that's never a bad idea,' Lil encouraged her.

'What about your schooling and all those exams and what not?' asked Mavis.

'Yeah, yeah, I'm going to be a good girl *and* do some of those CSEs, *and* keep my nose clean.'

'But you're still riding that terrible machine then?' Lil had noticed Peta's red helmet sitting on the side near the kettle.

'Yep!'

'We were that sorry to hear about that poor boy . . .' Lil lowered her eyes and stared into her cup.

Mavis nodded her head 'What a shock for you, you poor child. What a shock!' she added.

'But I was glad it wasn't me!' Peta confessed simply.

'Amen. Amen.' All three sipped tea in silence for a moment or two.

'So. You comin' back to us or not?' Lil asked finally.

'Nah, not much point. I'll be leaving again soon.' Peta took her cup to the sink and swilled it.

'What you aiming for now? Tech or what?'

'What, little ole me?!' Peta laughed.

'Well why not, with all your gifts and talents.'

'What talents and gifts are those then, Mave?'

'You know very well what I'm talking about. You think of Janie and all you done there . . . don't you ask me what your talents and gifts are! You know what you got inside.'

It was the first time Peta had felt miserable in a long time but she straightened up, looked Mavis straight in the face and said: 'Well, who knows. Maybe there's something out there somewhere. Got to be away from here, that's all I know.'

Mavis looked at Peta, 'Come over here, girl. Let me hug you.'

'God, Mavis, sentimental ole you!' But Peta submitted to her embrace and hugged Mavis back tightly.

'Hey! Don't be leaving me out here in the cold!!' Lil complained. Mavis and Peta parted to pull her into their hug too and the three of them stood in the middle of the office, hugging and laughing and crying a little.

*   *   *

Peta stopped for a moment to glance at the scale model of a Harrier jet which hung in the RAF display window. It was easier for the RAF and the navy to make an interesting show. Poor old army could only manage a case of badges, bagpipes, a drum, crossed swords and a bugle: all strangely in conflict with the modern images of fighting men projected in larger-than-life photographs behind the display cabinet.

No point in lingering. There was nothing relevant to her there. Up the marble stairs, through the double glass-doors. Turn left for marines and the RAF, straight on for the navy and then right for the army. There were two women in the room, sitting behind desks arranged symmetrically on opposite sides of the room. The overall impression was one of order and efficiency: the furniture serviceable, neatly arranged, the display material informative and accessible. The portrait of the Queen was in the exact centre of the wall beneath the clock.

'Can I help you?'

With great relief, Peta noticed the absence of hostility in the officer's eyes. True, she was a professional and trained to give nothing away behind those rimless glasses.

'I want to join the army.'

'*Ah!* Sit down.'

The woman's upright posture, accentuated by her well-cut lovat-green jacket, made Peta sit rather more formally than was her habit. She had made up her mind, she wanted only to sign the form and get cracking.

But it was not quite as simple as that, the woman explained. 'How old are you?'

'Seventeen years and three months,' Peta lied, having read that much in the careers base.

'Which branch are you thinking of?'

She hadn't realised . . .

'Oh yes . . . twenty-four jobs to chose from!' The officer passed a glossy brochure over the counter to Peta.

'Gentle in manner, resolute in deed!' Peta read. 'Special Intelligence . . . Clerk . . . Kennel Maid . . . Military Policewoman . . . Cook . . . Driver . . .' her eyes flicked down the contents page. That would do.

'*Driver!* I'd like to be a driver.'

'Ah, that's interesting. Why did you pick driving? Do you like to drive?'

'Got a bike. I like moving around . . . and I've driven my dad's car!' Annoyingly Peta felt herself flushing.

'And what about hobbies?'

'Hobbies?'

'Yes . . . what do you do in your spare time?'

'Well,' Peta thought, 'there's the bike as I said . . . oh

yes, I help out up at the hospital with mentally handi-capped . . .'

Surely she was on to a winner there but the woman said nothing, merely nodding her head and looking as though she was waiting for more.

'And . . . well, I like trees . . . you know . . . sitting in trees and thinking.'

'Ah that's good!' the woman said unexpectedly, 'There's quite a bit of hanging around for a driver, you know, driving something from A to B, then a long wait before driving back again.'

'Sounds OK to me. When can I start?'

This time the woman actually laughed. 'Not as easy as that I'm afraid.'

First, a simple form for a parental signature – Peta bit her lip – then an application form, a couple of tests, a medical, a further two-day interview and then, if she passed all that, a short delay then finally the start of the training.

Peta stood in the porchway at the top of the marble steps, her hands full of brochures and forms. It was raining. She crammed most of the papers into the inside of her jacket. Fortunately there was a biro in her top pocket and she sat on the step and let her eyes skim over the form: I hereby give permission for my son/daughter to proceed blah blah blah blah . . . Signed:

She took the pen, and with well-practised skill scrawled her father's signature, Tom Piper.

Prepaid, no need of a stamp, post it in the first box she came to. Pulling up the collar of her jacket and hunching her shoulders she stepped on to the pavement.

A lone figure stood looking in from outside at the window display. He looked puzzled by what he saw; he was frowning, but stood closer to the glass trying to get shelter from the guttering. David. What was David with his peroxide quiff and his pierced ear, doing studying the photos of heroic fighting men?

113

'Can't see you in a green beret somehow!' She stood behind him so he could see her image in the glass too.

'Oh, I don't know,' David replied. 'You been bunking off? Haven't seen you for a couple of weeks,' he went on.

'Been at my nan's mostly.'

'Oh . . . Nance! How is she?'

'She's great.'

'Anyway what are you doing here?'

'I asked you first!' Peta told him.

'No you didn't. You just said about the beret!'

'Ah well, same difference. Got time for a coke at Skipper's?'

'OK.'

Skipper's was certainly a 'low dive'. Its cheap tea, coupled with the notorious indulgence of 'Skipper', its proprietor, drew in all the down and outs of the town. Recently, he'd bought a pinball machine and Space Invaders and the bar had started to fill up with noise and the younger unemployed. Now he sold slightly less tea, and slightly more coke.

The rain had eased off again, and David and Peta actually found themselves an empty table, still full of dirty crockery. Someone had written 'Sod off' in mustard on the oilskin cloth. Peta piled up the plates as Skipper threw her an old cloth.

'The things I do for you, Skip!'

'And the things I do for you eh?' he said, handing her two cans of coke. 'Eighty pence.'

'Oh I thought you meant . . .'

'Get away!'

'Get a straw!' David called.

'A *what*?'

'I always think I'm going to cut my lip!!' he explained, pulling back the metal tag.

'God. You never change!' Peta laughed.

'Nor do you!'

'Oh, that's where you are wrong,' she told him. 'It may not show but I'm growing up and getting away from it all. I'm going into the army.'

'I always knew you'd end up in the army!' David told her, confidently.

'How did you know'? Peta asked suspiciously. 'I didn't know.'

'Just knew!' he said airily.

'I could have been a wrestler.'

'Or a road mender!'

There was a pause. Peta started doodling with the ketchup bottle.

'Anyway, can't see *you* as a lean mean killing machine . . .' she went on. '. . . Remember that frog we had to dissect? You *fainted*!'

He laughed. 'Oh, it's my mum! Keeps on about job security and tiptop training. I want to do catering you see. I've got a place already to do hotel catering and management at the tech but I promised the old dear I'd look into the army.'

'Catering! I can just see you now in a chef's hat in some fancy hotel or other . . . I know, what about the navy? Catering in the navy, that would suit you down to the ground!'

It would have hurt from anyone else but somehow it was always like this with each other . . . no threat, no malice. Just understanding.

Peta put the finishing touches to her portrait – a quiff of mustard swirls and a brown sauce earring. She signed it in ketchup. 'There!'

David laughed.

'Oi! What a mess and what a waste of all my ketchup. Kids!' complained Skipper. 'No wonder they're hanging round here all day . . . I'd kick you out if you lived at my house, perish the thought!' He pulled the tea-towel down from his shoulder, about to wipe down the table top.

'Hey! Hold on! That could be worth millions one day!' Peta told him.

'What would I do with a million eh?' Skipper retorted, smearing the yellow with the red and the brown. It was raining again and the cafe was filling up now with damp and smoke and noise.

'Let's go!' They both stepped out into the downpour with a perverse sense of enjoyment. Neither had any protection and soon Peta's hair was hanging in dark rat's-tails, and water was dripping off the end of David's nose. It felt good marching along the empty pavements while everyone else hugged the shopfronts and canopies or hurried along, their heads down behind umbrellas.

'*I'm singing in the rain – Just singing in the rain,*' sang Peta lustily, crashing her feet, still in old Mr Massey's brogues, in all the puddles. At the end of the High Street water was gushing out of a broken gutter pipe above the DIY shop, splashing on to the paving-stones below. Peta immediately went and stood under it, the full force of the water falling on her head. It thundered down, blocking out all other sensations.

David stood, laughing at her but more at the expressions on the faces of the passers-by. Eventually Peta stepped forward, water still coursing down her clothes, and dripping from her sleeves and trouser bottoms.

'Ah! That felt good!' she told David.

'It looked it.'

'Hey, all that blond's washing out of your hair man!!' For a second David raised his hand in alarm but then saw the mischievous expression in Peta's eyes.

'Where are you going now?' he asked.

'Do you want to come home with me? Biffo and Amy will be at school.'

'I'm a bit wet!!'

'Yeah!'

'What about your mum?!'

'Oh, you know what she's like about you – get away

with murder!'

Not a thought that had ever occurred to Peta, still, she was OK was Mollie, and besides, Peta was hungry and Mollie always insisted on feeding her. She fell into step beside David.

'She's not bad, your mum!' she told him.

'Not if she's your mum!' he said with feeling.

Peta laughed. 'I like her. At least you know where you are with her,' she said thoughtfully.

The Gibbs' semi-detached looked comfortingly familiar with its neatly clipped privet hedge, and the front path flanked by a line of rose trees. A yellow bike lay abandoned on the front lawn.

'Come on, better go round the back.'

Mollie was back there in the kitchen bending over the clothes basket, unloading a tangle of damp washing. She straightened up, astonishment on her face. 'Good grief! Just look at you two. Not an ounce of sense between you. Why in heaven's name didn't you wait till the rain stopped.'

Already the clouds were breaking up and the sun was shining brightly through the south-facing kitchen window. 'Honestly Peta, I'd hug you if you were dry, love. I am glad to see you, honest, but my God, the sight! You get out of those sodden clothes before you catch your deaths!'

David walked towards the door to the hall.

'And you're not moving from this room!' she called after him crossly. 'I'm not having pools of water all over my house!! Take them off here. I've got to wash the kitchen floor anyway as it happens. I'll fetch your clothes . . . God help me, I've never seen the like!'

Both stood in their undies at opposite ends of the room, feeling pretty sheepish. 'Here you are then. Hope they fit,' said Mollie as she threw each of them an assortment of dry clothes. 'Get your knickers off David, and towel yourself dry.'

'*Mum!*' he protested.

'Oh pardon me! Mr Modesty all of a sudden. You two, who used to bath together and I don't know what!' she laughed but did allow them to retire upstairs to privacy.

Peta emerged in a red sweatshirt of David's with a white G on the front and a pair of Don's trousers which wouldn't do up.

'Are you hungry?' Mollie asked them as they entered the kitchen.

'Yeah,' replied Peta.

'No,' replied David.

'He *never* eats,' Mollie complained as she placed two huge bacon sandwiches in front of Peta.

'And look at him, and then look at me!!' Peta told her, taking an enormous bite out of the bread and letting the grease ooze down her chin.

'Puppy fat! And anyway better fat than not eating at all. He'll get anorexia, I tell him!'

'*Mum!*' David protested again.

'Well, it's good to see you Peta, I must say. Been away haven't you?' Mollie asked her.

Peta nodded.

'And where did you two meet up again anyway?'

David flashed Peta a danger signal which she received too late. 'The army place.'

'Oh!' she spun round, a big grin on her face. 'Good boy, David. I sent him down,' she explained.

'Yeah, he told me!'

'Oh he would. I expect he told you what an old nag I'd been . . .'

'Yeah!'

'Oh, David.' Mollie shot him a betrayed look, then softened. 'But what did you find out anyway? Spill the beans.'

'Not a lot.'

'Why not?'

Peta decided to rescue him. 'I whisked him away before he got to the door I'm afraid. Anyway, I think that tech course sounds great!'

'You do?' Mollie sounded doubtful.

'Strikes me as a funny thing to want to do though, catering, if you don't like eating,' continued Peta wiping her place clean with the last piece of bread.

'Oh I do eat . . . it's just Mum!'

'Mum's cooking more like.'

'Well, food's not my problem,' said Peta belching.

Mollie disapproved of vulgarity but chose not to hear Peta this time.

'Anyway Peta,' she persisted. 'What were *you* doing at the army place?'

'Oh just turning an idea over,' Peta replied lightly.

'Oh Peta, no!' Mollie's tone and her shake of the head said it all.

'But if you see my mum, don't you tell her!' Peta added quickly.

'Doesn't she know yet?' asked Mollie, shocked now.

Peta shook her head. 'I haven't seen her in ages.'

'I know.'

Peta looked at Mollie suspiciously, then rose abruptly from her seat. 'Got to go! I'll get the clothes back to you soon.'

'Oh don't go yet!' Mollie begged, but she knew it was too late. She put Peta's sodden clothes in a bag for her. Peta took them from her silently.

At the back door she turned and said, 'Don't tell her you've seen me, please.' And though Mollie said, 'No of course not, if you don't want me to,' Peta was unconvinced.

The rain was over. The streets were drying. At the pillar box on the corner of the street Peta stopped and felt inside her jacket. She smoothed the crumpled envelope, then posted it.

May 1987

Of course Mollie had seen Frances.

It was Mollie who found Frances the day after Peta had gone. Not that Frances wanted to be found really, yet she was glad when Mollie had appeared, her anxious face pressed against the window. Relieved. Mollie fussed and mothered and made sensible arrangements and Frances didn't have to do anything except, at last, let go and allow it all to happen. Mollie had been right . . . this was more than a friend could deal with. She needed help; she admitted that. Not the bottle. Not the make-up and the mask; not any more. And it was Mollie who found the therapist for her, who made the first appointment, who borrowed Don's car to drive her to the door and waited till she came out again. It was going to be hard, Frances knew this, hard and painful, but it had to be. She had to find herself first and then see what followed. Down this time; right down. No good pretending that her toes had touched the bottom if they hadn't. Down first, before up.

120

June 1987

Exams had started. Peta knew that all she had to do was turn up at the right time, do the papers and then she would be free. Annette had undertaken to make sure that she was at least awake in time to get to school on the mornings she had exams. 'The rest's up to you kid.'

Peta hadn't bothered to tell them about the army, even after she'd completed the tests. It didn't seem fair to raise their hopes too soon, at least that's how she rationalised it to herself. But, each morning, when she heard Annette throwing up in the bathroom, she raced downstairs to check the post before Tom could get there.

It wasn't that she couldn't bear the thought of '*it*' and felt she had to get away. No, on the contrary, she was quite excited, but she just couldn't stay there and get in their way.

She had made no alternative plans so when the letter arrived with the official crest on the envelope, addressed to Tom and asking for his parental sanction, she was relieved. She knew – the officer had told her so – that this meant she had been successful. 'Guildford, here I come!' she said, tucking the letter down the front of her shirt.

'*John Brown's body lies a mouldering in the grave*!!' she sang all the way to the maths exam. She even carried on singing as she marched down the aisle between the desks in the main hall until the invigilator told her to

121

'Pipe down!' and the whole hall erupted in a gale of disorderly laughter.

The exam over, Peta returned home, drew the curtains against the summer light and settled down to an afternoon's TV. How great it was to be at home when Annette and Tom were out. She could sing, eat sugar sandwiches and bananas and even leave the peels on the arms of the settee if she felt like it.

Annette was on a late shift and wouldn't be home till eight. 'Do yourself something in the microwave,' she'd instructed Peta that morning.

Peta lay stretched out on the settee, her boots dangling over the arm-rest, an ashtray perched on her chest, and drew deep and comforting lungfuls of tobacco as Roadrunner outwitted the nasty fox, Jerry ran circles round Tom yet again, and Popeye, with the aid of his spinach, beat Bluto and rescued Sweet-Pea and Olive Oil.

May 1987

The therapist's office had been sparse: two chairs, a desk and no pictures on the walls. Just bare magnolia. Frances had worn black ribbed trousers and a large mohair cardigan which she picked and pulled at throughout the session. She had worn no make-up. She had put nothing – not even Nivea – on her face since Peta had gone. Her nail-polish was chipped.

'Well, what happens?' she asked nervously, perched on the edge of her chair.

'You tell me,' he replied disarmingly.

'I mean . . . do you ask questions? Do I lie on a couch . . . or what?'

He laughed, 'No couch!'

'Well, I don't know what to say,' she started.

He opened his hands in a gesture which seemed to say 'I'm in the dark too.'

Then just as Frances was despairing of ever getting anywhere, she found herself sobbing and sobbing and beginning to blurt out little gobbets of pain.

'And now . . . I know, just when I've got started you'll tell me to stop,' she cried out in panic nearly an hour later.

'No no, indeed. Carry on,' he invited her, which she did until she ran dry suddenly.

He looked straight into her eyes.

'I don't want to say anything today, Frances,' he had told her, 'but I do want to see you again very soon.'

June 1987

Peta heard Tom's key in the lock. It was unexpected but she didn't move.

'Good God! What are the curtains drawn for? It's a glorious day! What are you watching? Children's TV?!'

'It's good!' she said defensively.

He stood uncertainly in the doorway and then settled himself on the arm of the sofa, removing, without comment, her banana skin. He appeared to be watching the screen intently for a moment or two and then became restless. 'Look, are you really watching this?'

'Yes.'

'Well . . .' he glanced anxiously at his watch, '. . . I really just dropped by to pick up my clubs and, while I was about it, I thought I'd use this opportunity to, well have a chat.'

'What about?' she asked not taking her eyes off the screen.

'Well . . . look, Peta, it's really hard talking against this noise!'

'OK,' she leant forward and lowered the sound but left the bright images flickering crazily over the screen. She continued to gaze at them, mesmerised. Tom swallowed his irritation. Oh well, might as well get on with it and get it over and done with. This annoyance made it easier somehow.

'I've some news for you Peta.'

'Ummmm?'

'Annette's going to have a baby.'

124

'Umm. I guessed as much.'

'How?' Tom was astonished. 'It doesn't show yet, does it?'

'She's been honking up every morning for the last month.'

'Oh I see. I hope she didn't wake you up.'

'I'm not complaining.'

'No, well – we – um – no – I,' he corrected himself, 'I didn't really know how you'd take it. I feel, you know, it might be hard on you, nose out of joint and all that.'

'God no! Good news dad.'

Tom lingered awkwardly, glancing every second or two at his watch, wanting to be gone, yet feeling he ought to stay.

'Can I turn the sound up?' she asked finally.

''Course it isn't due until about Christmas!'

'Can I?' Peta had her hand on the button.

'What? Oh all right, I suppose so, if there's nothing else you want to say!'

'Me?'

'Yes. You!'

She shook her head. 'No, not really.'

Tom stood up abruptly. This was a ridiculous waste of time.

'Oh, don't worry about the room. I'll be gone by then,' she added, though it was as an afterthought.

Tom sat down again abruptly. 'No, no. You mustn't feel pushed out. The baby can sleep with us for the first few months . . .'

'And then . . .?'

'Well then we'll think again,' Tom told her.

'Anyway – as I was saying – as it happens, I'll be gone!'

'Gone, but where?'

'Army college.'

'WHAT!!' Tom squeaked, looking for a minute like one of the cartoon characters he wasn't watching. His

125

eyebrows shot almost up into his hairline in amazement. 'What do you mean, army college?'

'What I said, army college. I'll be at army college. That's clear enough isn't it?' She turned and looked at him.

'No it is not!! I do not understand at all. Who says so? I mean, where did this idea come from?' and he ran his hand through his hair, leaving it sticking up like a brush.

She touched her head with her index finger, 'My idea. I said so!'

'But we haven't discussed this . . . this is the first I've heard about it,' he complained.

'What's to discuss? Anyway I only knew today, I got this letter!'

She reached into her jumper and pulled out the envelope which she handed to Tom.

'It's addressed to me!' he said indignantly.

'But it's *about* me. Anyway they just want your signature for some reason.'

Tom carefully unfolded the single sheet and read every word slowly, including the date and the address. He hadn't finished protesting, though Peta knew he would sign it in the end.

'Well,' his tone petulant, 'I must tell you, Peta that I feel rather hurt about this. Not even to mention it, let alone give the idea a proper airing. I mean, it's your future we're talking about here!'

Peta's patience was giving out. 'Come off it, Dad. Don't pull that hurt crap. I know what we're talking about. I know it's my future all right. I thought I'd take care of it myself. *Unlike my past*,' she added, and then wished she hadn't. She knew she had hit pain.

Tom slumped. She felt him sitting heavily there behind her, and she could no longer focus fully on the screen. His hand on her head was an odd sensation, like a weighty hat. It was a pressure, but a kind of benediction too, and it was warm. Tom was her dad after all. Unexpectedly Peta had to fight back a sudden wave of desire to grab hold of his hand in her own and kiss it and kiss it.

Tom stood up and quietly and without another word left the room. Immediately, Peta reached into her pocket for a cigarette. She needed both hands to light it.

June 1987

He didn't normally take the initiative. He would sit impassively waiting for Frances to talk and direct her own progress.

She was surprised when, before she had even drawn breath, he said, 'Today Frances I want you to talk about your son!'

His eyes held her gaze and somehow she did not look away, though she could feel the pleasure change through shock to fear. His eyes calmed her somehow. 'You've told me that he was three when he died suddenly and unexpectedly in his sleep. But I think I am right in remembering . . .' (he was always correct, even without notes to help him) '. . . that you mentioned in passing that that was not the last time you saw him. I would like you to tell me more about that other time if you will.'

He spoke gently as he always did, politely. He leant back, placing his fingertips together while still focusing on her eyes. He expected, no, he knew, she would be able to speak. It was time.

Frances felt cold suddenly and shaky. Automatically she reached for her shoulder bag. 'I'll have to have one . . .' she told him.

He nodded.

July 1987

With exams over, Peta found time hanging
rather heavily on her hands even though she tried to
make the smallest tasks stretch out to fill a huge space of
time. She took to riding her bike to a different news-
agent's each day, covering miles just to buy her
cigarettes. It was good to ride fast and move the air on
these hotter summer days.

She was still waiting, still in between, but the space
was a good one, full of blue sky and sunshine. They
were all waiting in a way. Maybe for different things,
but it seemed easier knowing they were all playing the
same game.

Peta knew that Annette's waiting might make her act
strangely. Although she developed no particular crav-
ings for anchovies and ice-cream or cold beetroot, nor
did she start secretly eating coal dust, which Peta had
heard from Mavis and Lil *was* possible, she did start
behaving oddly. She started hoarding strange things
under a dustsheet at the back of the garage. Wheeling
her bike into the driveway after one of her expeditions
one day, Peta saw that the garage doors were open and
from the inside came sounds of unusual exertion. She
popped her head round the door to find Annette
struggling with a small chest of drawers.

'What you got there?'

'Oh nothing,' replied Annette, replacing the dust
sheet briskly.

'Who are you hiding all this from? . . . Me?'

129

Annette looked guilty. 'Well, not only from you. Really. From myself, too. It's bad luck you see, but I just can't resist collecting things: I feel if I hide them, then it will all work out all right.' She put her arm round Peta's shoulders and led her back to the kitchen.

'Come on, put the kettle on. A woman in my condition should be made a fuss of,' and sank down into a chair at the table while Peta spooned coffee into two mugs which she rinsed under the tap first.

'Those clean?' asked Annette anxiously.

'Ish.'

They sat opposite each other while the summer sun beat through the open window. Annette's face was still flushed from the heat and the exertion. Peta had rolled her cigarette packet into the short sleeve of her Motorhead T-shirt. A blackbird was singing cheerfully from the lilac tree outside.

'You all ready for off then?' asked Annette.

'More or less.'

'Which?'

'Well. Washed my knickers!'

'Ah well, that's the most important job finished.' Annette wiped her forehead with the back of her hand. 'God, I don't like this heat. This pregnancy seems to make me sweat. I never used to feel the heat like this,' she complained. There were dark patches staining under her arms.

'Should wear black like me! Doesn't kill the smell though . . .' Peta commented, and sniffed her armpits loudly.

'*Peta!*'

'Well . . . if you must lug furniture about single-handed . . . Come on, let's take this into the garden.'

Tom had buried most of his garden under crazy-paving slabs long ago but Annette kept up the various tubs and pots which were now full of blood-red geraniums, multi-coloured petunias, trailing blue lobelia and white alyssum.

Peta tucked a cushion under herself and sat on the paving slabs while Annette sat on a white wrought-iron garden chair in the shade.

'I hate this garden,' Peta announced in a matter of fact tone.

'Do you? I always think it's rather elegant,' confessed Annette, not in the least hurt by Peta's honesty. She cast an admiring glance over her flourishing tubs and the satisfactory way the clematis was climbing up its new trellis.

'No good for a kid!'

'Oh no, I suppose it isn't. I hadn't looked at it that way.'

'I mean, if it falls on this stone, it'll smash its head in . . . there's no grass to pull up . . . and the flowers you're so precious about. And what about riding a bike, and having a dog?'

'Hey, hey! Hold on, aren't you jumping the gun a bit? Who said anything about a dog anyway?!' said Annette, choosing to ignore the truth of Peta's earlier comments.

'Got to have a dog,' Peta told her firmly. 'I always wanted one but, well, Mum put her famous foot down.' Annette smiled at her but said nothing.

'Anyway,' Peta carried on, 'what about this nursery?'

'No plans. Not yet!'

'Superstitious?'

'That's part of it,' Annette confessed; 'I've just got a few things which could be used but, well, you know I don't want to make it too real yet.'

'*It is real!*'

'I know, but, you know!'

'Well, if you could just bring yourself to choose a colour, I could paint up that chest before I go,' Peta volunteered.

Annette wavered for just a second before saying, 'That's a lovely idea Peta; let's get some paint!'

Emerald green was the choice, and Peta approved. She dragged the little chest out on to the patio and sanded it down vigorously to the bare wood. There was a half-used tin of undercoat in the garage and once she'd burst through the thick skin and released the glorious smell and oily-grey paint beneath, she set to work with the new brush Annette had bought.

By the time Tom returned home the transformation was nearly complete. Drawers, stuck up at odd angles, were marooned on pieces of newspaper all over the paved area, drying in the late afternoon sun. Tom, exhausted by the unaccustomed heat, flopped into a chair in a small shady corner and sipped a long whisky and soda.

'Well, ready for the off then?' he asked.

'More or less,' Peta replied, catching a drip of paint on her brush and smoothing over the surface with even strokes.

Tom swilled his drink round, making the ice-cubes clink against the glass. 'Said all the necessary goodbyes?'

She knew what he meant. 'I'll go tomorrow.'

He looked at her anxiously.

'I will Dad. I'll go tomorrow. There, how's that?' She stood back to admire her work.

'Certainly cheerful . . .' he laughed. 'Can't say I'd have chosen bilious green for a baby though.'

'It isn't bilious,' she said defensively. 'Anyway, better than pink or blue.'

'Well, I suppose it depends on the rest of the colour scheme,' he said guardedly.

'Canary yellow and pillar-box red,' Annette told him through the kitchen window.

'*My God!*' He put his hand protectively over his eyes.

'And there's plenty of other painting that needs doing Dad, so get busy,' Peta bossed him. 'Looked in your garage recently?'

'Can't get near the place; what with your bike and her

132

rubbish, my poor old car has to sit out in the street,' he retorted.

'Well . . . I suggest you take a look under that dustsheet, and get off your butt,' she told him.

'I will,' he promised. She looked at him, her eyebrows raised. '*I will!*' And Peta laughed at the squeak in his voice.

'Well . . . I didn't realise she'd got as far as collecting things together. Bit early isn't it?'

'No crib yet,' Annette told him quickly.

'Oh . . . no problem there! We've got my old crib. My mother gave it to us just before umm . . . Peter . . . er, the first Peter . . . was born. And then *you* had it,' he told Peta. 'Frances must still have hold of it!'

Peta stroked the back of her hand with the brush. There were still traces of green visible in the interior of the thick hairs.

'Don't use that old thing. Get a new one,' she said.

Tom missed the urgency in her voice but Annette caught it.

'Oh I expect Frances gave it away long ago,' she told Tom.

'No, no! She wouldn't do that. Not without asking me. No, no, she's bound to have it somewhere.'

Peta stabbed her brush back into the jamjar of turps and watched the clear liquid turn green again. The regular backwards and forwards motion of the brush calmed her just enough to conceal her agitation then, quietly excusing herself on the pretext of doing some last-minute packing, she went up to her room.

June 1987

Frances leant forward, folding herself round her body, and seemed to fix her gaze on a point somewhere between her knees and the floor. She talked in a low, almost whispered monotone.

'I suppose you might call it a dream . . . I don't know . . . but it wasn't like the other dreams I'd had, you know, the ones when he'd be calling for me and I'd run after his voice and then I couldn't find him, or I couldn't reach him, or he wasn't there, or it was the wrong child and not calling for me at all. You know the kind. Well, this one was different. It had a different kind of ending anyway. I heard him crying for me. I remember waking up. And it wasn't even the same house, you know. It was after I'd left Tom but I'd taken some furniture, including the toy cupboard, all the toys, for Peta.'

The therapist nodded as she looked briefly at him.

'Well, the crying that had woken me had stopped, but I heard footsteps and anyway . . .' she took a deep breath and then continued slowly. He was listening intently. '. . . I got to Peta's room and opened the door and there he was sitting by the toy cupboard, playing with his bricks.' She stopped, held in the trance of memory.

'And then?' he prompted her.

'I called his name and he looked up at me and I bent down and reached out to him,' she gulped and stopped again. Tears were trickling down her face.

'And did you touch him?'

She shook her head. 'No, no, little Peta started climbing on my lap, you know how jealous children are, and by the time I'd pushed her away – he'd gone!' She sank her head into her hands and sobbed convulsively, huge sobs which shook her whole body. It took some time for her to reach her next statement. 'I suppose that was hard for little Peta too.'

She cried again, but this time it was for all the pain and all the confusion.

July 1987

Taking leave of Tom was not hard. It was something Peta had done many times before and, anyway, she'd be back and, anyway, she was still asleep.

He knocked on her door at seven-thirty. 'Peta! Peta! I'm off to work. Sorry to wake you but I wanted to say goodbye.' She groaned, turned over and sat up and blinked vacantly at him. Awkwardly he approached her and kissed her lightly on the forehead. *It was years since he had done that.*

Annette was eating a plate of muesli, standing by the sink when Peta finally emerged, sleepily. She was in too much of a hurry to sit down. Her sister's dark blue maternity smock seemed to emphasise her pregnancy.

'Only two more weeks of this,' she told Peta. 'I'm hoping my digestion will benefit from the rest anyway,' she said, gulping down the last mouthful. Then she galloped up the stairs to clean her teeth, smelling of peppermint when she returned and threw her arms round Peta.

'Take care!'

'*You* take care!'

As Annette turned to go, Peta suddenly called 'Wait!' She turned back as Peta put her hand out to just touch Annette's protruding stomach. She didn't say anything.

First stop, kiosk to buy cigarettes and a postcard of a Horse Guard in his sentry box. Second stop, Post Office

. . . first class stamp and withdraw thirty pounds. Write the card to Nance: *'One day this could be me!'* Three exclamation marks.

Next stop, Mothercare, where there was nothing, nothing at all, just chocolate-box frills and flounces, blue nylon, easy-care sickly pinks and citrus yellows. Everything so expensive too!! A deviation from the original schedule to the charity shop. That one would do fine, in the corner, a simple Moses basket with a hood. Twenty pounds, leaving ten for petrol. Oh yes, and the flowers. Back to Tom's. Scrawl a quick note. *'Don't use the old crib.'* Put it inside the basket and leave it on the table.

On with the rucksack, on with the helmet. One deep breath and away! Stop at the hospital gates . . . always flowers for sale there. Big bunch of yellow daisies. How to carry them? Tuck them into her jacket. Blossoms tickling her chin. Drive slowly to the recreation block. Park the bike. Office empty. Put the flowers in the teapot; all but one. Into the main hall. Janie's there, in her gingham with the white collar, looking at nothing. Peta goes over and gives her the flower. Janie's staring at it as she leaves. Lil and Mavis see her and wave. They will think she's waiting for them, with the kettle on.

Just two more calls.

Just two more.

Frances, rising early, had swabbed cold-cream on to her face, washed it off again and blotted it dry. Then, watching the dry skin appear and crack like flaking plaster she'd applied a dab of Nivea to her forehead and nose. She had chosen a pleasant floral dress with a lace collar, then discarded it for a pair of white cotton trousers and a fresh green shirt. She'd removed her bangles and found her arm felt strangely light.

Having drawn back her curtains, she realised with disappointment that it was a grey and overcast day, a different season from yesterday surely. It wasn't actually raining, but the clouds looked threatening and the wind was scattering the petals of the overblown roses. Pity – the sunlight was more cheerful somehow, more relaxing and now a green blouse and white trousers seemed wrong too. She changed again into her blue tracksuit.

In the kitchen Frances made herself a cup of coffee and slid the cake she had made on to a plate, which she placed centrally on the table. Next to it she put two plates and two cups and saucers. She'll know I've made an effort at least, she told herself, examining the cake proudly. It was dark and rich-looking with almond halves placed prettily in the top, just like shop-bought.

She took her coffee through to the front room and lit a cigarette and tried not to look out through the net curtains to watch the street for Peta's arrival, but couldn't help herself. Three times she went to the lavatory. She smoked three more cigarettes, emptying and washing the ashtray each time she did so.

'I know. I'll clean the bath,' she thought, 'that'll make her come . . . I'll listen to "Morning Story", that'll do it!' she told herself, peeling off her rubber gloves. 'I'll get involved in the story, and then she'll come and I'll never know what happened!'

The fifth cigarette and another cup of coffee she took into the garden, chilly as it was. 'She's not coming! *She's not coming!!*' she thought, and bit the inside of her cheek until she tasted blood.

'Hi!' Peta was standing at the back gate in her leathers, having just removed her helmet.

Frances quickly wiped her face.

'How did you get in?'

'Sneaked round the back!' she grinned. 'What are you doing in the garden?'

'Oh, just taking some fresh air,' Frances replied vaguely.

'I thought you thought fresh air and you didn't agree!'

'Oh well, all things in moderation! Come on in, I've made a fruit cake!'

'A *what?*' Peta followed her mother into the kitchen. She swung her rucksack off and put it down on the work top with her helmet.

'Wow!!' she exclaimed. 'Did you *really* make that?'

'With my own fair hands!'

'How motherly!'

Frances managed a faint smile at that as she searched for her sharp knife. 'Here, *you* cut it!'

'I don't like to. It looks so pretty.' Peta told her.

'Don't be so daft, it's meant to be eaten.'

'It looks as though this is some kind of celebration then,' Peta said, sitting back and taking her first mouthful, and looking intently at her mother.

'Well, is it?' Frances answered her stare.

Peta shrugged. 'I came to say goodbye.'

'I know,' Frances said evenly, pouring the tea into two cups.

'Ah! Not such a surprise then.'

'No,' her mother admitted.

'Mollie?'

'Yes.'

Peta chewed thoughtfully on her cake, '. . . And you know about the army too?'

Frances nodded and nibbled delicately at the edge of her cake.

'. . . And you're not going to say what you think,' Peta surmised, correctly.

'It's your life,' Frances said with deliberate irony.

'I never thought I'd hear you say that,' Peta replied in the same tone.

It hurt. It hurt. But Frances didn't show it.

'So, I've come for a fight and there isn't going to be one, huh?' Peta asked her bluntly.

'No. No fight Peta.'

'What, let bygones be bygones and che sera, sera?' she

goaded.

'For the time being . . . for today anyway,' Frances knew her voice was weaker and had a tremor in it, and she knew that Peta had heard it.

There was a moment – Peta poised and strong – '*Attack! Attack!*' – but the moment passed with the hesitation. 'Well,' she sat back, 'I'll have another piece of cake then – one for the road.'

Frances rose eagerly to cut another slice. 'I'll wrap the rest, take it with you . . .'

'Oh, that'll make me popular with the girls!'

Frances smiled tightly, but she smiled.

Cramming the last morsels into her mouth, Peta rose 'Gotta go . . .' She caught the crumbs falling from her mouth, threw back her head defiantly and caught them again as she tossed them up into the air.

'You won't stop me. You won't stop me!!' thought Frances. Then, as Peta bent down to pick up her bag, Frances dodged forward and put herself between Peta and the door. Peta, surprised, took a step backwards. Frances put her hands on either side of Peta's face, pulled her daughter towards her and gently kissed her forehead, holding her motionless for several long seconds before Peta straightened up and blinked at her.

Neither said goodbye.

Frances stood at the living-room window lifting the net to get a clearer view. She saw Peta adjust her helmet, kick the bike into life, lift it off its forks and then drive off down the road. Without looking back Peta raised her hand, knowing Frances would be watching.

Just one final goodbye.